THE DEVIL AND THE DEADLY PEACE

TALES OF KHAGA

THE DEVIL AND THE DEADLY PEACE

TALES OF KHAGA

SINDHURA CHAMALA

First published in India in 2016 by Kiwi Books

ISBN 978–93–85523–57–1

This is a work of fiction. Names, characters, businesses, places, events and incidents are either the products of the author's imagination or used in a fictitious manner. Any resemblance to actual persons, living or dead, or actual events is purely coincidental.

Typesetting and cover design: Kiwi Books

Cover photograph: "Verona by night" by Przemyslaw Krystaszek'

Kiwi Books
an imprint of Dogears Print Media Pvt. Ltd.
Plot No 16, Housing Board Colony
Gogol, Margao
Goa 403601 India
www.cinnamonteal.in

For all the steps we took together
For all the stories we told each other
Hear me now, wherever you may be
Thank you for walking along with me

They call me the Devil in the Dark. His "invisible assassin" you don't see coming. And I am here now on his call, but he is no more. I know about your meeting with him last week. Is the Brotherhood ready to fulfill its promise to him? Work with me to uncover whatever it is that he called me here for.

By the lake where you told him to contact you this week, there is a rock waiting for your answer. You have till the funeral to decide.

—The Devil

1. Death and Suspicion

"You look tired."

The minister of Jalika commented when Angla entered his outer office late in the morning. The sun was bright and filled the room with a warm embrace as Angla eased himself onto a divan by the window. He wiped his hands on a white towel and accepted a glass of water from the minister with a murmur of thanks.

"All the arrangements for the funeral are in place. I oversaw most of the work as the chief is busy pouring over the plans for the Peace Events again. We had to pull many workers hired for the Peace Events off their duty to quickly arrange for the cremation ceremony and the honoring dinner."

The minister nodded and watched Angla gulp down the water. He poured some more into the glass and walked back to his desk to put down the jug. He stood there for a moment, hesitating, and then moved around to sit in his chair.

Angla watched him silently and when the minister didn't say anything for a while, he ventured softly, "You suspect foul play?"

The minister sighed. "I do not suspect anything yet, Angla. But the king's death, a mere week before the signing of the treaty, does put some worrying thoughts in my head. And then there are the Events we are hosting to honor the peace and trade with both the nations. It's a delicate position that may get tipped over anytime."

"So what do you intend to do?"

"For now, wait. The prince will arrive shortly and then the king's body will be moved to the visiting hall. The council will be called to convene after the cremation and we shall meet shortly before we proceed to dinner. Before the meeting, I need to discuss with the prince about the crown. Meanwhile, I have asked Vaidyana to examine the body. We should get some news by nightfall."

Angla wasn't surprised; Vaidyana was in charge of the Medica. But before he could respond to the minister, the minister's squire, a young boy of fifteen, knocked on the door and stepped in. He nodded in recognition to Angla and spoke to the minister.

"Sir, I was told to inform you that an envoy from the First Nation has arrived and the chief of guard requests your presence at the East Gate to welcome him."

The minister frowned and threw a quick look at Angla. Then he turned to the boy and said, "Tell Nayak that I'll be there in a few minutes."

The boy quickly nodded and stepped out, disappearing into the corridor on the right. The minister started tidying himself up immediately while rapidly speaking to Angla.

"I knew a representative would be coming ahead of the officials but did not expect him to be here almost a week before the Events. He couldn't have known about the king's death till this morning, so he must've already been in transit. Whether the First Nation just wants to keep an eye on the preparations or they suspect trouble, I shall know when I meet him. You be on alert, Angla, and let me know about anything that catches your attention, even if it seems small."

Without waiting for Angla's response, he rushed out after the boy, leaving Angla to lock up the chambers.

The minister rushed out from the inner palace and entered the pathway towards the East Gate. His squire ran forward and informed him that the prince had just arrived and had headed straight to the Medica to see the king's body. The minister nodded at the boy and dismissed him before meeting with Nayak, the chief of guard, at the end of the pathway.

"When did you receive the message?" the minister questioned the chief without showing any hint of annoyance he felt inside.

"In the early hours of the morning," the chief answered him tightly. "But we didn't expect him to arrive until tomorrow. I planned to mention it in the council meeting today."

At that moment, the East Gate opened and two guards stepped in. They were followed by a well-dressed but weather-worn couple along with two others who looked like the couple's handmaid and squire. They were followed by two other guards, who, as the gate closed, stepped away to stand on either side of it.

"Welcome to Jalika." The minister schooled his expression to be gentle as he clasped the envoy's hands in a friendly gesture and smiled at his wife. He introduced himself saying, "I am the minister of Jalika," and pointed to Nayak, "He is the chief of guard." He then continued, "The prince has just arrived from the mines and is with his father along with the family. He excuses himself for not being here to welcome you."

"Very pleased to meet you," the envoy said. "We are sorry for your loss and our poor timing. My name's Merin and she is my wife Adola. We know we haven't given a fair notice of our arrival, so please excuse us for placing this burden on you at such a difficult time. We wouldn't want to intrude on any of the ceremonies. We will pay our respects to the king when visitors are allowed and then retire to our rooms. Please give our condolences to the prince and his family."

"Of course," Nayak said, stepping into the conversation. "I will show you to your rooms where you can freshen up. I've alerted the kitchens, and they shall send a meal to your rooms directly. When you are ready, you can come down to the visiting hall. We'll arrange for your meeting with the prince and the council tomorrow, if that is alright."

"That will be very fine, sir. Thank you very much for your generosity," Merin said. Gesturing to his wife and bidding farewell to the minister, he followed the chief toward the southern end of the palace to the visitors' bungalow.

The minister did not know what to make of the unexpected visit. The envoy visiting with his wife, together with a maid and a squire, might mean they had expected the visit to be spent in leisure, yet why arrive in such hurry when they weren't too keen on attending the funeral. He felt uneasy, and the feeling only intensified as he stepped on the pathway toward the Medica.

2. The Two Wars

The Little Brother locked the door to his loft and climbed down the ladder with a lantern in his right hand. The night was nascent and the wind was light. He stood at the bottom of the ladder and looked at the slowly emerging stars. It was a good night and it stirred up that sweet tinge of pleasure in his mind. Usually he spent such nights reading a book and smoking his pipe, both of which he carried everywhere he went. But he had already finished all the books he had brought with him to Jalika. He had been in Jalika for ten days now and the inactivity was getting on his nerves.

He opened the lock to the warehouse and entered it with the lantern held high. Placing the lantern on a small wooden table in the middle of the hall, he opened the windows to let the night's air in. Then he lit a few other lanterns that hung on the walls at different parts of the empty warehouse. He walked back to the table, sat in the chair facing the entrance, and wondered if his routine would ever change whenever he visited Jalika. The Little Brother, as he was called, being shorter and leaner than the other four Brothers, resented his presence in the group. However, it was the Brotherhood that had sponsored much of his travel and education over the seas when he was too young to have considered such opportunities and he was grateful to them for that. But he did not like being part of a group whose main objective was to ensure peace in Jalika when there already was the guard to do just that.

He thought back to the first time he was approached; he had been only twelve at the time and had been fascinated when they told him that he was a descendant of a family of the Brotherhood and so should be a part of the renewed one. They told him about the First War, the one that took place about two hundred years ago. He hadn't known much about it, except that it was so bad that the islands had lost more than half their population to it and that it was responsible for the establishment of a governance of sorts. The conflict was between Bora and Wisali, the two regions of the largest island among the small number of islands that constituted Jalika. These two regions were connected by a small stretch of thick forest, north of the backwaters separating them. People on both sides lived apart and there was often competition between the two for fishing and exploring the surrounding water and land. With time, the competitiveness festered into jealousy and hatred, and when a small fight broke out on a nearby smaller island between two men, it soon transformed into a fight between the two regions.

People from Bora and Wisali attacked each other any time they came across the other on the waters and both the regions started to lose their precious few rafts and the fishing boats to the attacks. Finally, the people of Wisali made a clumsy stone bridge across the water between the two regions and stormed into Bora to strike them on land. The people of Bora retaliated. The bridge grew strong and the attacks got more frequent. People from either side had to learn combat skills and stand guard for protection. It adversely affected the islands and their livelihood, and when huge ships, which they later found out to be carrying explorers from the Second Nation, were spotted circling the waters around the islands, the elders from both the sides sat down together. They came up with an agreement to leave each other alone in their respective regions of land and water. They made rules for trade with each other and with any new folk that may arrive and agreed to adhere to them under any circumstance. They declared the bridge between Bora and Wisali to be a safety passage for everyone and installed keepers to ensure peace for the both regions. Thus, the Brotherhood came to life.

For years, the Brotherhood guarded the bridge, settled minor disputes, and oversaw trade with the folk from mainlands. The bridge was later built to great strength and increased width, enabling people to move between the regions quicker and with comfort. There was much movement between the islands as well as with the mainlands of the two nations once the ports were established. The nearby islands were all brought under either Bora or Wisali and the region came to be known as Jalika, with Bora and Wisali as two main centers of trade. Bora, being the closest to the mainland of the Second Nation, had main trade routes open up with them and Wisali established trade routes with the First Nation. People focused on fishing, hunting, farming, small scale mining, and trading and soon old fights were forgotten. With sustained peace, the Brotherhood vanished into the realms of a forgotten legend, even by their own descendants.

The sound of steps brought the Little Brother out of his reverie. He walked to the door to see three silhouettes walking toward the entrance of the warehouse. He recognized the Elder Brother's tall, lean frame walking in the front. He was followed by the Second Brother and the Fourth Brother. He saw the Third Brother locking up the gate behind them. As they smiled at him and patted him on the back, the Little Brother remembered their first meeting again. He had been struggling to cope with the death of his grandmother who had raised him after his parents' death. It was the Brotherhood that had pulled him out of his despair and gave him a direction to focus his energy. He had been alone in the house as his grandmother's faithful helper, an aging man of sixty, slept outside, when the Brotherhood came knocking on his door.

After telling him about the origins of the Brotherhood, they had also talked about the recent war, which had taken place thirty years ago, the one that led to the initiation of a leader in Wisali, who marched his people into Bora to defeat the Evil Merchant and his henchmen. The war ended quickly and both the regions were merged into a single kingdom under the rule of Wisali's leader, who became the first king of Jalika. But it had been a bloody war and the two great kingdoms of Khaga, the First Nation and the Second Nation, had come close to attacking the islands during their time of vulnerability to capture its rich resources. So, the elders in the Brotherhood families decided it would be best that the Brotherhood came into operation again. The Elder Brother had told him then how they could've foiled the Evil Merchant's plans that led to the war and how they could've prevented the death and violence. Each member of the original Brotherhood family had been picked but he wasn't inducted earlier like the others because his grandmother had opposed the idea. They had told him that since he wasn't physically fit to be out on the streets with them, he was to educate himself and learn the ways of life outside Jalika, to come back and help them when necessary.

He never questioned their judgment and went where they sent him. He travelled the nations, staying for a while wherever he could through the relations in the Brotherhood families. He met many strangers, learnt various phases of Khaga's history, studied cultures and societies, and read as many books as he could his get his hands on. But every time he visited Jalika, his idea of the Brotherhood changed. He now saw them as a group of idealists trying to hold on to a forgotten tradition just for the sake of it. Jalika had progressed well after the war. The dead king had been a brilliant ruler, and under him and his council members, Jalika had two fully functional palaces, a guard, and two prospering treasuries with separate trade with both the nations. And when the Brotherhood had made contact with the king a week ago to let him know of their presence, he had been equally baffled too, which resolved the Little Brother's decision to finally leave the group. He wondered whether that night, their third meeting in the month, they would finally see light on his opinions. He went inside and cleared out the table as the Brothers entered and locked the door.

The Elder Brother looked at each one of them and asked, "Shall we start?"

3. A Prince's Dilemma

Nigam entered his quarters in a few quick steps and was greeted by his wife at the door to their private room. She had left the Medica earlier than him to give him privacy with his sisters and had already finished freshening up. A huge wooden closet, which hadn't been there the last time he visited, stood in the corner beside the mirror. He quickly undressed and entered the bath as his wife moved towards the closet. When he stepped out a few minutes later drying his face with a white cotton towel, he saw his wife arranging jewelry on the bed with her small, pale hands. The closet door was half-open, revealing a couple of empty wooden shelves and a couple more filled with more jewelry. Shaking his hair dry, he asked her what she was doing.

"Remember when I told you and the king about my interest in making jewelry?" she asked him, looking up from her work. "When I expressed interest to be a part of our family's work towards Jalika's prosperity?"

"Yes," Nigam said walking towards their wardrobe, "It was over dinner, wasn't it, when I was here the last time? Father was pleased."

"Well, yes," she answered, watching him wear a white cotton tunic and an old grey vest. "We need to embrace other royal customs from around Khaga as we will soon be under everyone's notice for hosting the Peace Events. So, I've collected some drawings from trading merchants of different regions and hired smiths to make some jewelry. These are my tribute to your father. I am taking them out to find some somber pieces for the dinner tonight. I'll hand a few pieces over to your sisters as well."

Nigam finished dressing and looked at her. He noticed how she handled the pieces with care, as if she was reverent of their making, and remembered how glad the king was that his daughter-in-law found an avocation that also promoted Jalika's interests. Nigam didn't think his sisters would be interested in jewelry of any kind, but they too, like their father, worried about her. He too was glad that she found something to keep her busy; he had always felt that she resented her life in the palace, though she had never shown any outward signs of it. He liked her, but his passion was elsewhere. He had been fascinated by the mines when his father had first taken him along on one of his many expeditions and had fallen in love with them after spending a few days with the miners many years later. With his father's permission, he had picked up the craft and lived by it ever since, staying away from his family most of the time. The miner in him would never let him leave for long the small islands where he worked day and night. He loved the cold, dark, and delightfully inviting caves where he slept and the dangerously unpredictable volcanoes by which he worked. He sighed deeply as he bade farewell to his wife, who looked up once again to watch him leave. He rushed through the door, worried at the realization that he may now have to take over his father's responsibilities, at least for a considerable amount of time to come.

He walked through the small door from the inner palace and entered the visitor's hall where his father's body was laid out on a raised platform in the center. Visitors walked around the platform in a never-ending line. He saw the minister at the other end, standing directly opposite the door, and walked toward him. He murmured a greeting as he stood beside him. He knew they needed to talk prior to the council meeting. But before that, he had to receive condolences from the people of Jalika who had come to pay their respects to his father. He leaned down to the minister's ear and told him that he would visit his chambers a few minutes before the meeting and saw him nod in return. Then he turned to thank the official who came to greet him.

He noticed his sisters entering the hall a few minutes later. His elder sister Nimoga was still crying lightly. Her husband placed his arm around her for support while she dutifully murmured her thanks to the many people who walked toward them. His younger sister Nigara stood on the other side of Nimoga, a little apart from the couple. She looked defiant and only nodded to the people without saying a word. Her stubbornness brought a smile to his face. Their father had great plans for her. He knew she was shocked a great deal. She didn't expect her first night of vacation at home to be her last with their father. She was still young and inexperienced and had just started the training their father had arranged for her in places all around Khaga. If only his elder sister was interested. But she, like him, never enjoyed being a royal. She loved her plants and herbs, a liking she inherited from their mother. And she loved living in the Second Palace, far from the Main Palace in Wisali and its royalties, on the edge of the largest plantation in Bora, where her husband was in charge of the treasury.

Nigam stood in the hall for a long time. After he saw the minister leave and the visitors thin, he thanked the last of the grievers and stepped out. But before he took more than a few steps, he was stopped by the chief of guard Nayak, who was not one to waste time on pleasantries.

"I hope you thought well about the succession, Nigam. It is not a matter to be easily influenced by misguided advice."

Nigam smiled at the chief and said, "I have given it considerable thought, sir. But as you know, I have been away for long and am in need of knowledgeable advice. But it is for me to judge the intentions behind it and let me assure you that no decision will be taken without the council's approval. I only ask for your faith in my judgment."

"Yes. Of course! You are inexperienced yet, but I do not doubt you." The chief looked uncomfortable with the realization of his haughty words and took his leave quickly saying, "I will meet you with the council."

***

The minister was at his desk smoking a pipe and deep in thought when Nigam entered his office a few minutes later. He sat in the chair across the desk and declined when the minister offered him another pipe from a deep wooden box. They sat silently for a moment and would've remained that way for long if it weren't for the time pressing on them.

"Have you spoken to your sisters?" the minister asked.

"Yes, for a little while in the Medica, but nothing concerning the palace affairs. But I have to tell you that they both assumed I would take our father's position now."

"Nigara is to leave after the Peace Events and it would be best if we do not disrupt those plans. And you know your elder sister better than I do, I don't expect that she or her husband would be pleased to consider leaving Bora. That just leaves you."

Nigam sighed and said, "Nimoga is with child." He smiled lightly as the minister's eyebrows rose in surprise and continued, "And my dear brother-in-law is already ready to leave. If it is up to him, they will not be returning for the Peace Events at all, considering how distressed Nimoga is with father's death."

"He is a good man, but he would never leave Bora. Also, we cannot afford to lose such an honest man from the Second Palace. We need people we can trust there and it would be difficult to replace him."

"What about you?" Nigam asked. "Have you not considered the position for yourself or for anyone else?"

"I was considering retiring after the Peace Events," the minister answered. "Besides, it would cause displeasure with some in the council. They may have supported your father unanimously but they would have trouble supporting each other. It would be best if one of your family members continues."

"You are right," Nigam agreed. "But I detect worry in your tone. Is there something I should know?" he asked the minister with a penetrating look.

"I am not sure, Nigam," the minister answered, returning his gaze. "For now, you worry about the council and the palace affairs and leave my suspicions to me."

"All right then," Nigam said and stood up. "Let's proceed to the meeting."

4. A Deal with the Devil

"We do not know anything about the identity of this person?" the Little Brother asked, curious for the first time.

"Apart from the letter, there is nothing to establish his existence," the Elder Brother answered, noting the Little Brother's interest. "But he mentioned our meeting with the king in the letter and that makes me believe its validity."

The Little Brother was certainly intrigued. He picked up the letter that the Elder Brother had dropped on the table and read it. "He says that he's called the king's Invisible Assassin. Has anyone heard about him?"

"There were many rumors about the king at any time," the Second Brother recalled. "In his thirty years as the ruler of Jalika, he has done much. No other kingdom in Khaga has even established trade with both the nations together, and it was his idea to keep the two trades separate within islands. Because of this, Jalika has not only continued to become prosperous but is still on good terms with both the warring sides, or they wouldn't have agreed to the peace treaty."

The Third Brother nodded in agreement and said, "There is said to be rivalry within the council and yet he guided them well in settling many issues in the islands. And I think he was supported by several people over the course of his life, but he keeps his relationships tight and his plans in the dark."

"Though it was his idea to raid Bora thirty years ago, he was known to have shown reluctance in starting the attack," the Elder Brother added. "It is also rumored that he stopped such situations many a time, both before and after the unification of Jalika. It is possible that he engaged an assassin to eliminate a few people rather than lose many in a battle."

The Fourth Brother, who took the letter from the Little Brother, looked up and said, "We haven't heard anything on the streets so far and the king didn't seem too troubled when we met him that night."

"This Devil says that he wants us to work with him to uncover something that the king called him here for", the Little Brother examined, "It could turn out to be anything at all. But the king obviously told this Devil about us even after we asked him to keep it a secret, so we cannot discount the relevance of his words."

"You don't think someone could have found out?" the Elder Brother asked.

"I doubt it," the Little Brother answered. "We took painful measures to reach the king undetected. And we were alone with him in his inner quarters, to which no else has access. Even if someone saw us, how would they know about the Brotherhood? Unless one of us told someone about it, I don't see how anyone else would know. Not only that, he also mentioned in the letter that we should leave an answer at the meeting spot we mentioned only to the king."

"We have a deadline. The funeral is tonight," the Fourth Brother spoke when everyone was silent.

"When did you receive the letter?" the Second Brother asked, looking at the Elder Brother.

"I received it today morning. My neighbor's three-year-old daughter brought it to me when I was feeding the cattle in the backyard. She said some lady at the well told her to give it to me. When I questioned her about the lady, she just said that she was a nice lady."

"So what do we do now? Do we agree to a deal with this Devil?" the Second Brother asked when everyone was silent again.

"All he seems to be asking for now is collaboration," the Elder Brother said, looking at everyone. "I don't see any harm in saying yes to that. Let us see what this brings to us. But we should investigate the identity of this person to be sure."

When everyone slowly nodded, he turned to the Little Brother, "I know you feel restless and want to leave soon. But I advise you to stay here for a little while more, at least till the Peace Events. If there is any evil plot brewing, that is when it will be served."

"You are not good in a fight like the rest of us," the Second Brother said. "You should be extremely careful and work in shadows."

"Yes," the Elder Brother agreed. "For now, you will be responsible for the communication with this Devil and finding out about him as much as you can. If you agree to it, you can start by leaving our answer at the lake tonight."

Everyone looked at the Little Brother expectantly, waiting for him to object like he did to any task he was offered in the earlier meetings. But he silently nodded and got up, leaving the others surprised.

The Little Brother lit a new pipe before walking out into the night. He was feeling wonderful, walking alone in the streets of Wisali with thoughts running wild in his head. Since his childhood, he was fascinated with mysteries. While the other children got into trouble or caused mischief, he silently followed and observed the elders. If something intrigued him, he would try it on his own or would simply put it away in his head, ready to be recollected when needed. There were very few things that held his interest for long, but whenever he would take up something new, in the beginning, the excitement would get so overwhelming that he could barely control himself from shaking.

A few years ago, he never would have expected anything like the Devil in Jalika. Life in Jalika was simple; everyone concentrated on their profession and left the others alone. The palace quickly settled the only problems that arose—the need to hold ownership of mines or forest areas. Due to the prosperous trade and the king's ingenuous request to both the nations of Khaga to exempt Jalika from the impending war, the islands rose to prominence. Once the peace treaty gets signed in the Peace Events, the popularity of Jalika would only grow. But, to anyone wanting to harm either of the nations, the Peace Events provided a perfect stage. The Little Brother wondered what the next few days would uncover.

He walked off the main street and entered the small narrow lanes, coursing through them quickly towards the lake. The Devil intrigued him. He was also interested in the trouble the king might've suspected that led him to call the Devil to Jalika. Until more was revealed, he would concentrate on the Devil.

As he caught sight of the lake straight ahead in his path, his eyes darted around, noticing the presence of every hut and every tree nearby. It was hard to miss the rock the Devil referred to in the letter. It was at the north end of the path where it turned right around the lake and disappeared into the thick forest. On it, the Little Brother found the symbol from the letter.

He walked toward it and looked around to see if anyone was looking in the general direction of the rock. But there was no other movement save the light breeze that gently ruffled the leaves. He picked up a lime piece that was near the rock, wrote the Brotherhood's answer beneath the symbol, and took a deep breath.

5. The Council

Angla locked the minister's chambers and handed the key over to the waiting attendant in the small open area outside the office, who got up from his wooden desk to take it from him. Once the assistant had gone back to his desk, Angla made his way to the kitchens for an early meal. He then headed to the gardens to meet with the guards to be stationed at the cremation. After that, he spent some time in the visitor's hall speaking to Nayak and other officials. When he saw the minister gesture to him and leave, he too left the hall immediately, caught up with the minister for a few quick words, and then walked toward the east end of the inner palace. He stopped at one particular bend in the corridor, looked around to make sure no one was present, climbed up the roof, reached his secret spot, and waited patiently for the council to start.

He had found the spot while inspecting the store room next to the council room one day. There was a gap on the roof, very close to the ventilator on the wall separating the two rooms. On his way to his quarters from the workshop that night, he had climbed up to the roof to investigate it. The gap was in a corner, a little to the left from the pathway to the East Gate, and out of sight from the guards stationed at the gate as well as from the guards posted at the end of the pathway. The other side of the corner was blocked from view by the coconut trees marking the end of the gardens. He could climb up to the roof, sit a few feet inside on the low edge connecting the two slanting rows of tiles and he could become invisible to everyone in the palace. He came there often to sit quietly and think.

As he waited for the council members to arrive, Angla thought about his conversation with the minister before the prince had come to visit him. The king's death was caused by breathlessness that stopped his heart. Given his age, it seemed to be the most likely case of natural death but Vaidyana had asked the chemists to check further. Angla knew Vaidyana well; she wouldn't have asked the chemists if there wasn't a strong reason in her mind. She was rarely in doubt, but when she was, she would do everything to remove it.

Vaidyana was the youngest on the council. She had been handpicked to become the chief of Medica by her predecessor when he wanted to retire. She was the most patient and kind among the council but she was fiercely protective of her patients and extremely careful with her treatment. As she told the minister, Vaidyana had directly examined the king's body after the death and had detected rashes along with other indications pointing to consumption of bad fish. But for a meal to bring death it either would have to be a large fish that only dwelt deep in the sea or the king would have to have had an unusually large amount.

Angla heard voices. The council members had started arriving. He heard Hosam, his parched barking voice acquired by doing disputable and sometimes dangerous experiments. But he was responsible for discovering many useful combinations of the minerals found in the volcanic rock formations, some of which helped Vaidyana in healing and Banomar, the weapons master, in his forging. Hosam was highly respected but people avoided him on principle and only dealt with him when there was need to enquire about chemicals. Usually all such enquiries are catalogued, but Vaidyana had asked Hosam to keep it under wraps on the minister's request. This had troubled the chemist because accountability is a highly regarded precaution in the palace of Wisali. Hosam had agreed only after a personal request from the minister, but he had warned that it would take a long time to be completely sure of anything and that he would put it down in the books if he discovered anything unusual. But time was something they did not have, and that was the reason the minister had called Angla aside and asked him to look into the matter of the king's death discretely. Angla had wanted to attend the council meeting to gauge the members' movements but his chief, Nayak, had been already throwing them both angry looks. So they had decided it would be best if they didn't attract much attention to their investigation. They needed Nayak to be focused on the security for the Peace Events more than ever.

The council meeting commenced once all the twelve members including the notary arrived, but Angla had trouble listening for a while as the breeze grew heavy. By the time he was able to focus, the minister was already talking.

"... keep this short and we shall meet again soon," the minister was saying. "But tonight we just have the matter of the ascension to the throne."

"Whose ascension, we wonder," Nayak said in a clipping tone.

Angla knew that Nayak and the minister never saw eye to eye, but he had never heard his chief being caustic. Nayak considered the minister to be too superficial as he had spent the better part of his life on interests like collecting art or studying cultures. Despite the king's explanation about how, over the years, the minister's network of relations brought an advantage to Jalika, Nayak felt that he should have never been made the minister. And Nayak, of course, hated that his second, Angla, was mentored by the minister and still maintained a close relationship with him. Angla sighed over his predicament and concentrated again.

"... will return after the Peace Events, and I think it is better not to interfere with my father's plans for her," the prince was saying in a rather low voice, "and my elder sister and her husband plan to return to Bora soon."

"You are right. We should wait till Nigara is ready before we consider her for the throne," agreed Rahugmana, the treasurer of the Main Palace.

"The current ascension will be temporary and we shall review again in seven years unless the chosen person decides to step aside earlier," the minister announced, and from the ensuing silence, Angla understood that everyone had nodded in agreement.

"I have asked the minister to consider the position," the prince said and Angla was surprised that Nayak did not burst out loud, "but he has declined it in league with his planned retirement." The prince continued, "He has also advised that someone in the family should take father's position as it is only temporary and would not cause much disruption to the plans laid out for each of you for the Peace Events as well as for the near future."

"What have you decided?" Nayak asked in a much gentler tone.

"I will do it. I shall be the king until my sister is ready," the prince said in a louder voice, "And if no one has an objection to this, we shall quickly take a vote."

"I am happy with your decision and hope that everything will be smooth with the Second Palace as it was with your father," Irany, the primary of the Second Palace, mentioned quickly to which the prince must have nodded because then there was silence and the notary announced the Council's agreement about the next king.

The prince would make a great king if only his heart was in it, Angla thought. But he had always preferred physical labor to people and politics.

"When should the crowning take place?" Vaidyana queried. "It has to be before the Peace Events."

"And we should also consider establishing royal protocols." Nayak put forth his thoughts, "Your father established the palace and its workings, but he preferred to run it like a home rather than an office. We cannot afford to continue that as we are no longer just an isolated group of islands."

"Yes. Privacy and guard cannot be dealt with lightly in Jalika anymore," Vihoro, their spokesperson with the foreign courts, agreed.

"We shall discuss upon these matters in the next council meeting. Tonight we honor our dead king," the minister declared in an even tone.

"Alright then, I shall meet you all in the gardens in a short while," the prince concluded the meeting.

6. In the Interest of Weapons

Angla stayed in his spot even after the council meeting ended. He heard general talk and scraping sounds as the members got up to leave. Nayak was discussing dispatch of a weapons shipment to the Second Nation with Banomar. The Second Nation must have gotten wind of new orders from the First Nation to have placed another quick order after their earlier one from less than a month ago, Angla thought.

Jalika was new to weapon trade but it already had all the three manufacturing units working at full capacity. Before the war thirty years ago, both the regions supplied raw material to many kingdoms. But when the Wisalis attacked the Borans with their fishing tridents and hunting needle blowers, the nations took notice of the incredible ideas of the clever minds in the region. With the resources available in the islands, it was easy to manufacture weapons in Jalika on a large scale and export them. The weapon's master was a brilliant huntsman and knew how to design deft weapons with youngsters like Angla providing him new ideas from the field.

Weapons were what attracted Angla the most as a kid. As the ruler of Jalika, the first thing the king did was start schools. Experts in each field were asked to volunteer to teach, and if he or she could not leave their respective place of stay, the interested kids travelled to their teacher. As a tall, strong boy, Angla was asked to join the physical training. He was agile and he learnt the movements promptly, but it was his quick thinking and clever tricks that won him fights. It came to him easily. He was always fascinated with weapon making, and he focused his energy on it while practicing his fighting skills. He used to sneak into the wide shed—which both the minister and Banomar had used as their workshop many years ago, the minister for working with his minerals and his craft and Banomar for his trials with different models of weapons—and observe for hours.

Angla's parents, farmers in a small village, were worried that he wouldn't return home much. But they soon realized that their son's place was with the palace. He forged a strong friendship with both the minister and Banomar that endured time. The workshop for weapons had grown and Angla had his own space to work. However, as he was not experienced enough to introduce weapons of his own, he needed Nayak and Banomar to judge his models before they were tried out in the training. Once declared fit, the weapons would be examined by Kaliki, in charge of the trade, who looked at everything according to the interests of the kingdoms in trade with Jalika.

Angla got down from his spot and entered the pathway leading to the inner palace. He stepped onto the corridor on the right, making his way to the West Gate. The palace was a widely spread, rustic building with two levels below and two levels above the ground and symmetrical on either side of a four-hundred-year old stone temple. It was simple yet brilliantly crafted with proper ventilation and light on all levels. The palace had long halls and wide spaces; all connected with huge corridors on the inside and shaded pathways on the outside. The part of the main building around the temple, referred to as the inner palace, consisted of a long court hall, a treasury, a small garrison, the council room, several meeting rooms, private rooms, inner chambers, in addition to quarters for all the royal family members and the council members who chose to stay within the palace. Just surrounding the inner palace were the visitor's hall, the court hall, several consulting rooms, and outer offices of the council members. The stables, warehouses, a large garrison, three large workshops, quarters for soldiers and other workers, guest houses, and a greenhouse surrounded the main building within the perimeter besides the gardens, a small stream, and large grounds on all sides.

The Medica was a huge building with its main area and a few treatment rooms within the perimeter of the palace. But a large portion of the building was outside the wall on the left side of the West Gate that was used to attend to patients from all over Jalika. There were many important buildings both on the west and the south sides of the palace, just outside the perimeter. On the east side of the palace, after the gate and the palace wall, was a large ground used as a training station for the soldiers. A small village and a large port harbor with offices overseeing trade, fishing, and other operations existed beyond the training station. The northern wall of the palace ran at the end of the gardens, in between several rows of coconut trees. Outside the wall were huge plantations, some under the control of the palace. Several council members had houses close to the palace, mostly in the main town southwest to the palace wall. There was a huge ground outside the West Gate, which was also the main gate, with a large stage used for major events. At the end of the grounds was a market covering almost the entire western edge of the grounds. The region towards the north of the outside grounds was filled with several manufacturing units, a prison, a school, warehouses for the market, and many quarters.

As he entered the long south corridor of the palace, Angla caught sight of Vihoro walking toward the stables. Angla lifted his hand in greeting and saw Vihoro smile at him nervously as he walked past the corridor's edge and disappeared behind the stables. There were three two-storey buildings a little in the back, behind the stables with a beautiful view of the grounds, the port, and the ocean behind. Angla guessed that the visitor from the First Nation was accommodated in one of the buildings, and that it must be where Vihoro was headed. He turned at the end of the corridor, took the three steps to climb down, and walked toward the main entrance of the palace building where he stopped to speak to the extra guards posted there.

The entrance faced a large pathway from the main gate and was lined with tall Asoka trees that kept the way well-protected from the sun. He turned, entered the grounds, and made his way to the workshop next to the soldiers' quarters. He nodded at several people making their way to the gardens for the funeral dinner and politely declined when they asked him to accompany them. He was in no mood for a gathering today. He had a long day ahead the next day with tasks for the Peace Events, preparations for the crowning ceremony, and the investigation that the minister had asked him to undertake besides his everyday work. But he knew that he wouldn't fall asleep early even if he tried. So he decided to work on the small lightweight arrow that he had started to model for which he had recently received the raw material.

Several people moved around in the yard outside the workshop, but no one bothered him as he walked past it. He went straight to his room on the left end of the long hall and opened its lock. When he realized that he had left his tools in the stock room the last time, he ventured back into the hall and walked to the stock room that stood closed across the hall, exactly opposite his room. He opened it with his personal key, left the door open in case he needed to collect more material, and returned to his small room. He removed his shirt and set to work.

A couple of hours later, he heard a distant, shrill cry and stopped his work. His back was aching and his eyes were tired when he straightened up from his work bench. He stood still listening and heard the cry again. It sounded like a child's cry but he wasn't sure; it could've been a bird, and no children were let near the workshops. He dropped his tools and walked to the window. He saw no one except for the trees standing tall in the dark. Realizing that it was late, he put his shirt on and stepped out of the room to lock it. He heard the cry again, milder than before as if it was muffled, and ran the length of the hall to look outside the door in the yard. Seeing no one except for the single guard standing near the entrance, he walked towards him and asked if he heard any child cry nearby, to which he got a negative answer. Convinced that it must have been a bird on one of the trees outside his room's window, he turned back and locked the workshop. He warned the guard to be on alert and asked him to notify him immediately in case he heard anything. He then walked to his quarters to rest.

7. The Lost Brother

It was still dark when the Little Brother woke up in his small room. He quickly cleaned up, wound a towel around his head to stop the cold from entering his ears, and set out to the lake. He walked straight to the rock where he had spent a long time the night before waiting for the Devil to come. When no one did, he had headed home to catch a few hours of sleep before returning.

As he stood facing the rock, he noticed a tiny movement on top of it, directly above where he had written the answer the night before. He climbed up easily, finding footing in gaps among smaller rocks, and saw that an irregularly torn piece of parchment was placed on the rock with a small stone on top of it. There was just enough light to see that it was a message to the Brotherhood. He looked around and saw blurry shapes moving about; people had just started coming out, some in groups and some individually. There was no one nearby and no one seemed to be headed in the general direction of the rock. He quickly picked up the parchment and climbed down. He then walked toward the house of the Elder Brother, who lived close to the lake, and knocked on his door.

The house was large with a wide corridor that ran along the length of it and was only broken by the steps that lead to the main door in the front. A little while later, the Elder Brother, naked except for the plain cotton grey trousers, opened the door. His eyes went alert looking at the visitor. Nodding to someone inside, he stepped out, closed the door, and led the way to a small storeroom asking the Little Brother to follow him. It was dark inside the room when they stepped in, and the Elder Brother left the door slightly open to let a thin shaft of the morning light in. He then turned to the Little Brother and asked, “What is it?”

"It's a message from the Devil. I went back to the rock after only a couple of hours sleep, but someone got there before me." The Little Brother handed over the parchment to the Elder Brother who held it towards the light and read it out loud.

"Man the bridge and its crossers while I find out information in the main towns. Find out if there have been any unnatural deaths in the tribes. Strangers like me are not very welcome there."

"You are heading back again?" the Elder Brother asked, folding the parchment.

"Yes," the Little Brother answered.

"Let me get you some food."

They headed outside and the Little Brother waited just outside the house as the Elder Brother went inside. He returned in a few minutes with a small package of food wrapped in a cloth.

"I will let the others know," he informed the Little Brother as he handed over the food package. "We will leave a message at the warehouse if there are any developments."

"I will check in at sundown if possible," the Little Brother said.

"Be careful and do not head into dangerous situations alone," the Elder Brother warned him. "Make sure to leave us a message if you cannot meet."

The Little Brother nodded and headed to the lake. This time he made his way around the small colony of houses and emerged at the edge of the rock lining the lake, which ended at the turning into the next village.

The Elder Brother was the only one who lived close to the Main Palace and far from the bridge. The Second Brother lived and worked in the Second Palace in Bora while the Third Brother lived in the village next to the bridge in the region of Wisali. The Fourth Brother lived in one of the smaller towns of Wisali, somewhere between the Third Brother and the Elder Brother. The warehouse where the Little Brother stayed was close to the Elder Brother's house and was their only meeting place in Wisali, which they rarely used. They were known in the area and did not wish to be seen together. So they mostly met in a tree house in the forest that was neither in Wisali nor in Bora, but close to the bridge, at the northern end of the backwater from the sea that separated the two regions.

The king had chosen the lake as his meeting place with the Brotherhood as it was mostly deserted at nights, and he often took walks there alone. The lake was surrounded by thick trees and rocks except for two small openings, one giving an entry from the village the Elder Brother stayed in and the other from the small town through which a main road ran straight to the north end of the palace. It provided a perfect cover if one wanted to stay hidden.

When the Little Brother reached the lake, the sun had already risen and he could feel the morning rays warming his skin. The place was crowded with people, some carrying water, some fishing, and some offering prayers while the little ones played around in the mud. At the turning where he emerged, a few kids were playing under a large neem tree. There also was an old, ragged man leaning on the trunk of the tree, watching the kids from under his half-closed lids. He looked like he hadn't moved for a long time and didn't want to for a long time. Wondering if the old man had spent the night there, the Little Brother approached him to ask if he had seen anyone placing the parchment on the rock. He greeted him and when the old man didn't respond, he leaned forward to tap on his shoulder lightly.

"He is asleep, do not wake him," one of the little girls warned the Little Brother.

The Little Brother looked at the man and saw that he was indeed asleep. His eyelashes were so thick that it looked as if his eyes were half-closed.

"Who is he?" the Little Brother asked the kids who stopped playing and gathered around him in a semi-circle.

"He is a beggar but he calls himself a wanderer," one boy offered.

"He sleeps here once in a while and the noise doesn't bother him. But he gets annoyed if someone wakes him up," another boy added.

"Have you seen anyone else here today? Anyone you don't see every day?" the Little Brother asked the kids, keeping an eye on the mothers at the lake who started throwing him suspicious looks.

"No, just you," the girl who had warned him earlier replied cheekily.

"We came here only now. No one else comes here this early." Another girl who looked older than all the others answered him.

Figuring that he wouldn't be getting any answers there, the Little Brother walked towards the lake to drink water. He then settled down to eat on one of the rocks shaded by the trees, but this time on the other side of the opening to the lake.

8. News from an Old Friend

The Little Brother asked people at the lake if they saw anyone around the rock. After receiving only negative responses, he went to the rock to see if he could find some clues. But the ground around the rocks was covered with thick grass and no prints could be seen. He turned and saw that the old man had now disappeared, and it was just the kids playing. He had believed that he would notice if the old man left, but surprisingly the old man had disappeared without a sound.

Realizing that his investigative skills outside of books and facts were close to nil, the Little Brother went to visit one of his old friends who lived in the village. As it was still early in the morning, his friend was home and the Little Brother asked him to keep an eye out for an old man who slept under the tree near the turning to the lake and report his activities. He then caught a bullock cart making its way to the market and got onto it in the back. He reached the market at the peak of its rush and waded through the small spaces to find the lane he was looking for.

The market's small streets were lined up with everything that could be found, grown, or made on the islands. Since the market was the largest in Jalika and the closest to the palace, it had many foreign visitors and had shops especially for the items the visitors would find interesting. Apart from the general market of fruits, vegetables, and the like, there were metal shops that supplied both raw metal and carefully crafted artifacts. There were also shops with seashell crafts and other earthen and ocean crafts. The Little Brother passed through them quickly and entered the main market where the locals traded. At the main market, one could find shops for grains, herbs, farm tools, hand loomed clothes, diamonds and other stones, and shops setup by skill traders like seamstresses, smiths, and other craftsmen. Most people in Jalika, unlike from the places he had visited in other kingdoms, never paid by coin. They just made note of the debt and cleared it every few months either through barter or by a single payment.

He turned toward the oldest buildings in the market and approached his friend's shop apprehensively; he was never sure which one of the similar looking buildings was his friend's lair, where several men and women came together to sew clothes hour after hour each day. He visited rarely, and because the entire street was filled with only such shops, he could never be sure which one of them belonged to his friend. Just as he was about to enter the second shop on his right, which he thought was his friend's, he heard someone call him from ahead and turned. It was his friend waving at him from the stairs of a shop, third on the left from where the Little Brother stood.

"I thought this one was yours," the Little Brother shouted at his friend as he saw him walk toward him.

"It is. I was just up there chatting with someone," his friend said, giving him a hug. "Come upstairs. I've got a small personal room there now. What are you doing here?" He talked away in his usual fast manner as he led the Little Brother to the stairs. The ground floor was full of workers except for a small desk where his friend usually kept watch. He walked to the stairs at the end of the shop with his friend and climbed up. The stairs led to a wide room on the top with five more workers hand painting and block printing, and there was another small room on the side just after the stairs. The Little Brother entered the room and his friend closed the door behind them. They both sat down on stools near the window and his friend shouted at someone below on the street to send up two glasses of lemonade.

"Looks busier than usual, work going well?" the Little Brother asked.

"Yes, yes. But we've all got extra workers now to fulfill incoming orders."

"Large orders?" the Little Brother asked.

"Why, yes. Haven't you seen the new tunics? Everyone in Jalika has got one by now. It's for the Peace Events."

"What new tunics?" the Little Brother asked, dumbfounded.

"We've got paintings of Jalika on clothes, crafts, and even carts. It was a painting group's idea to sell their paintings to visitors during the

Peace Events, but everyone quickly caught on. Now, even the palace ordered painted tunics for all its workers. We even got special orders, someone wanting a specific island, a specific lake, or a specific building on their clothes. It has become a fashion of sorts, and if it's making us some profits, who are we to refuse," his friend laughed.

They heard a knock on the door and his friend got up to open it. A tall, lean teenage girl got two glasses of lemonade on a tray and handed a glass to each. She was wearing a short red blouse and a long green skirt of cheap silk, with her hair tied in a long braid. She smiled at the Little Brother when his friend introduced her as the daughter of a worker, who was spending time there to learn painting. The Little Brother smiled back at her and then she left, closing the door after her.

"So, how long are you here?" his friend asked. "Not off on one of your travel bouts soon?"

"I am here till the Peace Events at the least," the Little Brother answered. "I am running some errands for my cousins while I am here."

"Oh, the Peace Events. That is all everyone is talking about these days, except of course the king's sudden death. That really dealt us all a shock in the midst of the excitement."

"He died in his sleep, didn't he?" the Little Brother probed.

"Yes. Old age of course catches up with even the strongest of men."

The Little Brother nodded without an expression and commented, "Business must've boomed recently in Jalika because of the Peace Events. Everyone seems to be taking it well."

"Not everyone is happy, of course," his friend sighed. "Some people are extremely possessive of these lands and do not want foreign politics in the name of development. They had enough of that with the Evil Merchant in Bora before the war."

"Some people are not happy then?" the Little Brother asked.

"Not happy, yes. But they do not hold a grudge, seeing what it will bring to us; easy trade with many kingdoms and safety when both the nations go to war. That counts more."

The Little Brother nodded, talked a bit more about general life, and then got up to leave. He declined when his friend asked him to stay for lunch, but he accepted one of his newly painted tunics. He then left, walking slowly, trying to catch a glimpse of the girl again.

9. An Unexpected Visit

The Little Brother wanted to emerge on the other side of the market, towards the north western end of the palace grounds, and head straight to the school, fondly called Peettam. A little distance from the market, where the imperial buildings and the residing quarters ended, was a small village that consisted primarily of farming families. Most of the families had at least one member working for the palace in some way. The school was at the northern end of the village, outside its borders.

But by the time he could wade through the heavy crowd of the market and its irregular lanes, he was hungry. He decided to walk toward the school through the village rather than the quarters, so that he could find water and shade for his lunch. After walking into the village on the main road for a while, he found a water pump. There were few houses on the lane a few paces behind the pump. The area was mostly deserted, except for one or two people walking at a distance on the road. There was a yew tree on the other side of the road and he decided to eat there. He washed his hands and face under the pump water and then crossed the road. He found a stone on which he could sit comfortably and opened his food package.

The Elder Brother had packed a large quantity of food for him, out of which a huge portion was still left after his breakfast in the morning. It was hot and sunny when he walked, but the spot where he was sitting was cool in the shade. He ate quickly but diligently without looking around much, only listening to the typical village noises. He was about to finish when he looked up to the sound of a horse. He saw a soldier on a tall black horse passing out of the village. The Little Brother was suddenly reminded of one of his friends who worked for the council in the palace. It was Katmayo, a friend he made when he had gone hunting with the Brothers. Katmayo was from the tribe that dwelled in the Chama forest, which started right after the school building. He remembered that Katmayo and his wife had built a house in the village and had moved in last year. Though the Little Brother never knew what his friend did for the council, his friend had once hinted that he worked for the minister. The Little Brother knew that the minister maintained a network of people—spies, messengers, and errand runners—and he reckoned that his friend must be one of them. As it would be mealtime at the school, he decided he would first visit his friend to see if he knew anything unusual happening inside the palace as the Elder Brother's contacts did not have much to tell.

He finished his lunch, cleaned up, and started down the road again. He soon realized that he had forgotten where his friend lived. Luckily for him, when he arrived at the village center, he found a group of old people relaxing and talking quietly. He made some polite inquiries and found out where his friend's home was. He backtracked a little on the main road and turned right. He walked straight till he reached the beginning of a paddy field and turned left. He knew it was his friend's house as soon as he saw the hut-like structure after two small buildings—it had a wild quality of its own that he always associated with his friend. He reached the small fence made with long wooden branches, thorns and twigs, built mainly to keep animals away from the small plants inside, and opened the small separated part. It was eerily silent as he walked up the small yard and knocked on the door.

He waited for a while and when there was no response, he knocked again. Just when he was about to turn back, he heard movement behind the door and it was opened. There stood a young woman about his age, who he realized was his friend's wife. He introduced himself as her husband's friend and asked for him. She stood confused at first, telling him that her husband wasn't home, but she soon recognized him from her husband's stories and smiled. She invited him to sit on a wooden bench beside the door while she went inside and got him a glass of cool water. As he returned the glass, he noticed that she was pregnant.

"You look just like he described you," she told him. "He told me about how he tried to teach you hunting and about one particular time when you were chased by a pack of crazed wolves as you accidently stepped in while they were eating."

The Little Brother laughed at those memories. She collected the glass from him and sat on the bench across from him, gently touching her stomach.

"How far along are you?" he asked her.

"Oh, six months," she said with a delightful smile.

"That's wonderful," he responded to her smile. "So where is Katmayo? Out on one of his secret errands for the palace?"

She smiled knowingly. "No, he is doing some preparation work for the Peace Events."

"Will he be back soon?" the Little Brother asked her. "I haven't talked to him in a long while."

"He will return late in the evening but he might not stay for long if he gets another assignment."

The Little Brother nodded and wondered, "Is he still disappearing through the nights? How long has it been? I never really asked him how it started."

"Oh, I think it was about seven years ago," she answered hesitatingly. "You know how the king liked to visit places in Jalika, the smallest of the islands, remote places in the hills, and even tribes in the forests like ours. Well, whenever he visited, he would bring along several officials with him who kept an eye out for skilled people and that's how they found Katmayo."

Sensing her apprehension, the Little Brother didn't press. He got up to leave and said, "Well, I shall leave now. I do not know how long I am here in Jalika, but in case he wants to meet me in the next week, I'll be staying above my cousin's warehouse near the lake." After she nodded to that, he added, "Do you need any helping hand here?"

"Oh no, no, thank you. Today was just an emergency, some additional plan because of the king's death. Otherwise, the preparations were done already and he is usually home to help me out."

"Okay then, take care."

He turned and left the same way he came, thanked the old men again at the village center, and continued on his way to the school.

10. The Quest Comes to an End

The sun was burning brighter than usual that noon and the Little Brother tried to walk under the shade as much as possible. At the end of the main road of the village, he took a right and walked the wide road leading to the school. The road was flanked by coconut trees and opened into a large dry ground. The school compound stood in the middle of the ground with a small entrance to the school through which he could see the main building at the other end. The guard standing at the opening eyed the Little Brother curiously as he walked past him. The ground inside was wide with occasional trees throwing enough shade for the kids to play. At the far end, on the left, the Little Brother saw a man with his back to a tree, sitting on a wooden chair. He was reading out loud to a small group of young girls and boys, who looked only a few years younger than the Little Brother.

He walked across the ground, climbed the flight of stairs onto the stone porch, and entered the main building through the wide wooden door. He was in a small corridor with a door straight ahead that led to a small garden. Behind the garden, he could see the rest of the building. On his right was a wide hall, which was empty except for a woman at the far end, filling an earthen pot with water from a steel container. On his left was a wall with a heavy granite plate with details on when the school was started and below it, written in lime, was the number of students currently in the school. There was a door beside the wall through which he walked in and entered a small room. The room had four desks and two long open windows on either side. Only one desk was occupied, the one beside an open window that overlooked the gardens. The young man sitting at the desk looked up surprised.

"I am sorry, who are you?" he asked the Little Brother.

"Just a visitor," the Little Brother answered. "I am looking for the registrar? He knows me."

"He is out for some work. Are you here for a student?"

"Not a current one, but maybe an old one," the Little Brother told him. "I'm afraid I do not have all the details. But it's essential that I find this person."

"I am sorry but I do not have such details, I have just started working here. If you wait, one of the elder teachers may come in. Few of them live upstairs, but I do not want to disturb them."

"No, that's not necessary. I will visit again. Thank you."

The Little Brother turned back disappointed. Today was not a progressive one, he thought as he left the room and exited the building. But he knew that it would be that way for the next few days. He smiled at the young kids who came to play on the porch and walked back to the compound wall. He looked at the guard who was still eyeing him suspiciously. He stepped out onto the ground outside when he heard the guard's voice behind him.

"What were you looking for?"

"Just news about an old student," the Little Brother answered, turning to look at him.

"Did you find it then?" the guard continued as he bent to retrieve something from his small bag.

"No. Why?" the Little Brother asked, his curiosity piqued.

"Here." The guard handed a rolled parchment to the Little Brother, "This is for you."

The Little Brother scoffed in surprise. He took the parchment and asked the guard, "You know who it is?"

"You will too, soon," the guard said and went to a small stool on the side of the entrance and took out his pipe. The Little Brother realized that he was more a spotter for the kids playing on the grounds than a guard. Having understood that he wouldn't be getting any more answers from the guard, he turned around and left. After leaving the premises to make sure he didn't show any emotion to the guard, he opened the parchment, read it, and smiled. He was going to meet the Devil.

***

Several hours later, he sighed in relief as he successfully picked a lock without making any noise or disturbing its inner workings. He wanted to master the art before leaving, and so tried even after the Devil had left. It was a first time parting gift, the Devil had said, to teach an art in stealth. He was disappointed at first, but the Devil had just smiled and showed him how it's done. However, that had been only after a thorough questioning on how the Brotherhood snuck into the palace and into the inner chamber of the king. It was already a known secret to the Devil that the Brotherhood visited the king and the Little Brother did not see a reason to hide the details.

He had told the Devil that the Brotherhood's little adventure into the palace to meet the king was mostly just careful planning on the Elder Brother's part. The Elder Brother's mother was involved in the construction of the palace and had spoken about it to him most of his teenage years. He also had friends who worked in different positions in the palace and he had gathered information from them over the years. So he could easily lay out the plan to reach the inner palace, but it was how to approach the king after that that was tricky. An old woman, who worked in the stone temple in the inner palace and with whom the Elder Brother used to stay when his parents were away, gave him the king's schedule for the day and the layout of his chambers.

***

They checked in early in the evening to the palace to attend the soldier try-outs that the palace had planned and regrouped late at night near the soldier's quarters. Then they all borrowed the guard uniforms and set forth to the palace. They used the dark spaces and unwatched corridors to get into the inner palace, which took them about two hours. They then headed to the temple and, from there, snuck into the little personal garden of the king. It was the Little Brother who had peeked into the room first and found the king studying on the floor beside the fire place. He ducked and informed the others that the king was yet awake. The Elder Brother then knocked on the door that led from the garden to the king's personal room.

A full minute later, the king slowly opened the door, wrapped in a shawl and holding a knife, which he didn't bother to hide. The Brothers bowed to the king, whose face showed an expression of shock. To relieve any alarm that might've been caused because of their unexpected presence in the inner room of the king, the Elder Brother immediately explained who they were and asked whether they could speak for a while. The king looked at them all then, one by one, from head to toe while his expression slowly turned into that of amusement. He then stepped into the garden and closed the door to his room behind him. He motioned them to a set of chairs laid out in the garden and asked them to talk.

11. The Sweet Trouble

Merin felt much better after a short nap. They had travelled as fast as they could to arrive early in Jalika. Their original plan had been to arrive in Jalika at least three days prior to the Peace Events to oversee the preparations and ensure the safety of the dignitaries, who would arrive only one day prior to the Events. They had been at one of the rest stations in an allied kingdom when they received some disturbing news. So, after a single afternoon's rest, they had to resume their journey.

They had arrived near the mainland port closest to the east port of Wisali late in the morning, the day before yesterday. They were to gather information while recovering their strength, before they headed out to the islands. But the news of the king's death had led them to set out once again in a hurry. Merin had decided that he wanted to be in Jalika as soon as possible to see if any ill plans were already in motion.

The dead king was a man of his word. He had been responsible for the First Nation's smooth trade with Wisali, both before and after the unification of Jalika. Jalika was a rich source of minerals, and ever since the weapons trade boomed, both the nations had continuously tried to make allies with the islands. The king had wisely stayed away from picking a side and had made a bold move by asking both the nations to sign the peace treaty. Both the nations had known that refusal would mean a trade cease, and that would make the opposition stronger. They could've attacked Jalika and forced them under their rule, but they knew it wasn't easy, given its strategic location. Besides, the Jalikans would not have gone down without a fight. It would have meant a loss of many people and resources, which would have left the attacking nation considerably weak. Moreover, maintaining a rule in the islands would have been difficult. So the two nations had agreed to the treaty after months of deliberation with the allies and even the enemy kingdoms. In return, the king had promised that Jalika would remain a neutral party and continue the unbiased trade with the warring nations. It was due to his wisdom, peacefulness, and loyalty to his lands, that the neutral parties that wanted the cold war to end had picked Jalika to host the Peace Events.

The First Nation didn't want war either, but they would be foolish to not be prepared. Merin had had a short conversation the night before with Vihoro, who had promised him a tour. So, he had woken up early, gotten ready, and stepped out from the huge bedroom onto the wide balcony where breakfast had already been arranged. He had left without disturbing his wife, Adola, and had instructed her maid to wake her up in a few hours. He had then come down to meet the soldier waiting for him with instructions from Nayak. He had taken his squire along with him and followed the soldier to visit the housing setup for the Peace Events. He had returned tired in the afternoon and had decided to take a quick nap.

When he woke up after his nap, he stepped out onto the terrace and saw his wife sitting underneath the shade of a big creeper. It was well spread on the long rods placed for its support. The chairs and the small table were moved from the centre of the terrace to below the creeper and lunch dishes were already placed on the table. His wife and her maid were admiring a bird perched on the edge of the terrace wall, just at the end of the creeper. They both turned as he walked towards them.

"I was just coming to wake you when we saw this lovely bird. Didn't you say that you would be meeting someone in the afternoon?" his wife asked him as he sat in one of the chairs. She sat next to him as the maid served them.

"Yes. Nayak, the chief of guard. We will go through the arrangements."

"Did you meet anyone in the morning?" he asked his wife, watching the maid go back to the bird.

"The king's eldest daughter, the one married to the treasurer in Bora. I met her just before the couple left the palace and asked her about news from Bora. She didn't know much about their dealings with the Second Nation. She looked worn out already and I didn't want to press her about anything with her husband nearby."

"And in the afternoon?" he asked her, nodding to the maid who came back to serve some more.

"I wanted to meet with the younger daughter but she seemed elusive," Adola answered. "I've heard from her sister that she's only spending time with her friends as she will leave soon after the Peace Events."

"I've heard she's too young to take the throne. I wonder if the prince will do it," Merin commented.

"I wanted to meet his wife," Adola told him. "She invited me over to her smithy where they make jewelry. I will go tomorrow."

"Tomorrow, Vihoro has planned a tour of the palace for us," Merin informed her. "Let her know that you will visit the day after."

Just then, they heard a soft thud and saw the bird lying motionless on the terrace floor. The maid rushed to it and the couple set their plates aside and got up. Adola bent down and saw that the bird was not breathing. Merin saw some brownish yellow substance on the wall where the bird was and reached for it.

"What is this, do you know?" he asked the women.

"It is the sweet dish," the maid answered. "I fed it a little bit earlier."

"The bird's dead," Adola declared.

"Do not touch it," Merin warned her and moved to the table. He lifted the lid on the only unopened dish and saw the same brownish yellow substance. He lifted the dish to smell it. It smelled of garlic; he wondered what sweet dish needed garlic.

"Could someone have poisoned it?" Adola asked in a whisper.

"We do not know anything yet," he told her. "I will go see Nayak now. Vihoro told me that only a few people knew about us and our stay at the palace. Yet it must not be difficult to find out. I will get this sorted, you be on alert."

He called his squire and told him to stand guard. Then he went down with the dish and told the soldier standing there to lead the way to Nayak's office. For his part, the soldier did not give any expression if he noticed the dish in Merin's hand. He was told by Nayak to lead Merin to Nayak's office after lunch, so he simply obliged. As he followed the soldier, Merin thought hard. It could simply be an accident. But he was in a foreign land without many resources at his reach. And he didn't see any motive for the few people who knew about his visit to hurt him. It would cause more damage to Jalika than it would to the First Nation.

They entered the southern corner of the palace, walked along the corridor till the end of the court hall, and turned left. At the end of the corridor, there were three steps climbing down into a small hall. The soldier walked to the far left of the hall where there was a narrow staircase leading upstairs. He motioned Merin to the stairs and waited. Merin went up the staircase and noticed that the soldier didn't follow. There was a wooden door on the landing, which he knocked once before entering.

Nayak was at his desk noting down something in a thick ledger. There was a wide, open window behind him through which dim light filtered in.

Merin walked up to the desk, pushed one of the two chairs aside, and placed the dish on the desk. Nayak closed his ledger and stood up surprised.

"What is this?" he asked Merin.

"This dish was arranged in our lunch, and a bird just died from eating a tiny portion of it. Care to explain?"

12. The Banned Surprise

"I want it tested for poison," Merin told the chief calmly.

"Alright, we'll take this to the chemists right away."

Nayak quickly stood up, locked his journal, maps, and other parchments inside his desk, and walked out asking Merin to follow him.

"We do not want to alarm anyone. So why don't we go see Hosam in his office? He has a small room behind his office where he could test this right away."

They climbed down the stairs and walked through the corridor opposite to the one Merin entered from earlier. The corridor continued a long way with many rooms and halls on its left. There were several openings to the right, each with three steps leading down to the yard surrounding the main structure. On one such opening, after what seemed like half the length of the corridor, they both stepped down and walked towards a small house where Hosam stayed. The house was shaded by huge trees on all sides and there was only one door leading straight into Hosam's dark office. The room was empty when Merin and Nayak walked in. Hearing their steps, Hosam came out from an inner room through a short, narrow passage behind the desk. He looked surprised at seeing them and Nayak quickly introduced Merin to him.

"Merin suspects that this dish was poisoned. A bird died after their maid fed this to it. Could you please test this?" Nayak asked.

"What?" Hosam exclaimed, and then he managed, "Oh, yes, of course."

Hosam glanced at Nayak nervously as he took the dish from Merin and then went back to his inner room. Nayak and Merin sat in the chairs in front of the desk watching him move around and mutter some ineligible words.

"Who knew about us staying there?" Merin asked Nayak.

"The prince and the council know that you are here. The minister, Vihoro, and I know that we've allocated one of the visitor buildings on the northern end of the palace for you, but only Vihoro knows which one. The soldiers guarding and the servants of course know where you stay but they do not know who you are."

"And the lunch?" Merin asked. "Our maid told me in the morning that two or three servants from the kitchens brought our meals."

"Yes, the kitchens are always informed of any guests. Only the main cooks, a couple who has been working for us for many years, are informed about the background of the guest in order to fulfill any specific needs. Unless told otherwise, they serve our regular meals to the guests as well."

Merin nodded and Nayak continued, "That is what is suspicious. We do not serve a sweet dish for lunch here, only for dinner. Moreover, the kitchens have been instructed about the customs of all the kingdoms that are visiting for the Peace Events. So, the couple knows that you don't have the habit of eating a sweet dish for any meal."

They heard Hosam close a cupboard door and watched him come out with a grim face.

"It's definitely poisonous," he said.

They looked at each other and then Nayak asked Hosam, "What is in it?"

"It's no poison or venom I know. It smells of garlic. I tested it for two of the toxic metals and I can take a guess, but I have my doubts. It's the poisonous mineral we found for the first time a few months ago on the island of Megala."

"Megala?" Merin looked surprised. "I've never heard of this island."

"Megala is one of our uninhabitable islands," Nayak told him. "It's barely big enough to be called an island. As the volcano there has been silent for many years, we have started operations on it last year."

"And this mineral?" Merin asked.

"It is a highly poisonous mineral that we found in small amounts in some deep caves," Hosam said. "It has two toxic metals that make it extremely dangerous to be handled. After only a few experiments, we have banned it from any use."

"Then how did someone get hold of it?"

"We have many unidentified places in Jalika and they could've gotten it from anywhere. In the palace, any requirement for banned substances has to be approved by the council and is carefully monitored by Rola, who manages the inventory at the workshop. I cannot reveal much information to an outsider but I can tell you that this substance was discovered only a few months ago and is not public knowledge yet."

Nayak gave Hosam a long look and Merin thought that there was much the chief was not telling him.

Nayak suddenly stood up, "I want to head to the kitchens and make some queries. Do you wish to come?" he asked Merin.

"Yes, certainly," Merin answered.

They bid farewell to Hosam, who stood nervously behind his desk, and walked towards the kitchens. They left the dish with Hosam, as he wanted to confirm his speculation. So they walked empty handed, both silent except for the sound of their feet on the gravel. They only walked a short distance when they met Adola along with Merin's squire.

"Are you coming from the kitchens?" Merin asked his wife.

"Yes," she answered. "I couldn't just wait."

"Well, what did you learn?" Merin asked her.

"Accident or not, it doesn't seem to be an attempt on us."

"What do you mean?" Nayak asked her, forgetting formalities for a moment.

"Most of the staff had just come in because of the long work they did for last night's dinner, but I spoke to the couple who told me they ran the kitchens." She looked at Nayak for confirmation.

Nayak nodded and said, "Yes. They must have recognized you. Have you told them about the incident?"

"No, I just made some polite enquiries about the sweet dish. They were surprised there was any sweet dish in our lunch and had to make their own enquiries around the place. The sweet dish was leftover from last night and they kept a little aside for the youngest princess, as it was her favorite. Our maid, who makes a regular appearance in the kitchens and is a huge blabbermouth, told anyone who would listen that she liked sweets, but Merin and I did not, which she begrudged. No one in the kitchens seemed to know how the dish got onto our lunch trays, but if it was on purpose, it must've been meant for our maid, maybe as a warning to us. Otherwise it was to poison the princess."

Both Nayak and Merin were shocked. Then Nayak said, “Thank you for saving us the time. I will soon get to the bottom of this.”

“You better do that quickly or no one from the First Nation or its allies are going to step foot on these islands, and that means no peace treaty either,” Merin told him.

“We are aware of the risks,” Nayak answered him calmly, though his jaw was twitching. “We will take better measures now. All the visitors and their housing will be monitored and the preparation of food will be carefully supervised.”

“All right then,” Merin said and then moved to walk away with his wife. “We shall meet again later to go over the plans, if you let me know a suitable time. Please keep me informed about this unfortunate incident.”

13. A Warning and an Advice

Angla heard a knock on his door and rose from his bed to answer it. It was Nayak, looking tired and grim. Angla was surprised; his chief had never visited him in his room. It was always somewhere else but mostly in Nayak's outer office.

"Sir, what brings you here?" Angla asked. "Do you wish to come in?"

"Yes," Nayak nodded. "I wanted to talk to you about something privately. It's a matter of grave importance."

Angla offered him a chair, sat on the edge of his wooden bed, and said, "You could've sent for me."

"I was at the workshop just now, and the guard there told me that he saw you on your way to your room. As it will ensure us privacy from any prying eyes, I decided to come here."

Angla nodded and said, "I was training the soldiers. I came here only a few minutes ago to freshen up."

"Are the arrangements going well?" Nayak asked.

"Yes, sir. We've got some extra people for the funeral work and have retained most of them in case of emergency."

"We might need them soon for the crowning ceremony," Nayak commented.

"It has been decided then?" Angla asked him, already knowing the answer.

"Yes, the prince has agreed to take the throne, at least temporarily. We will soon decide on the crowning day. I had a small chat with the prince yesterday night at the dinner. We will plan it for at least a day before the events."

"Preparations for the events are mostly done. We can organize the ceremony without a glitch with the extra strength we hired."

"Good."

Nayak remained silent for a minute before saying, "I didn't find you at the dinner last night."

"Yes, sir. I wanted some peace; I was working late in the workshop."

"What were you working on, the poisoned arrow you told us about?"

"I placed the order for some of the material required for the arrow. But, I haven't checked if we have received it yet. Rola wasn't present in the inventory room when I went in yesterday; he must have been at the dinner. So, I worked on building a lighter bow for easy handling that can be used by amateurs."

Nayak was silent again. He looked around, taking in everything in the room as Angla waited patiently. Something's troubling the chief, Angla thought.

Then Nayak said decisively, "The toxic powder you had ordered for the arrow was received yesterday by Rola. He placed it in the stock room in case you needed it. He also said that the stock room was open this morning when he arrived."

Angla looked shocked and said, "I realize it now, yes, I had forgotten to lock the stock room. I went in to get my tools but left it open in case I needed other material. I was distracted when I was leaving and forgot to lock it. What happened? Has something been stolen?"

"Yes, that seems to be the case. The toxic powder is missing. Rola found out that you were in the workshop last night. So, this morning, when he noticed the powder missing, he thought you might've taken it."

"Someone else must've taken it. I still locked the main door, how could anyone enter without a key?"

"Well, many people have the key to the main door, including several guards."

Looking at the surprised expression on Angla's face, Nayak explained, "It was a recent decision. It was lax of us to not inform you. Many things needed mending with all the preparations going on, and since most of you have personal rooms, access to the main hall was provided to several people in case the tools were needed."

"So we do not know who has taken it?" Angla asked.

"No. But it was mixed in a lunch dish served to the envoy from the First Nation."

Angla had been expecting news of that sort for a while then. Nayak wouldn't have come to his room just to talk about the disappearance. "Were they poisoned?"

"Fortunately, no," Nayak answered. "Their maid fed it to a bird and it died. They made enquiries immediately after. It was mixed in the sweet dish kept aside in the kitchens for Nigara, but was sent with the envoy's lunch. If it was sent to them on purpose, their maid was the likely target because the envoy and his wife don't eat sweet."

"Do you suspect me?" Angla asked directly.

"I did at first. Hosam told me straightaway that it was the banned poisonous mineral and Rola confirmed that the only order was yours. You were in the workshop late yesterday when everyone else was at dinner, and you had been to the stock room where it was stored. Vihoro told me that you saw him walking towards the visitors' buildings, so you could've guessed easily where the envoy was housed. But the same reasons also tell me that it might not be you. You wouldn't be so foolish." He sighed and continued, "You are a smart guy Angla, a keen hunter, and you never take the first strike in a fight. I watched you a long time before I recruited you to be my second, even though I knew you were close to the minister, whom I dislike. But my insight into you is not enough. Either you did this on your own or someone who knew you well did. I am leaving it to you to prove to me which is the case."

Angla returned his chief's gaze unwaveringly and answered, "I will, sir. How has the envoy reacted to this?"

"I have been warned to find the culprit soon or there won't be any peace treaty."

"I see. Who else knows about this matter?"

"Hosam and I, and I shall of course report this incident to the council. Vihoro and I shall continue to work with the envoy on the preparations, as promised, for our long-standing friendship with the First Nation."

"Will you be revealing the complete details to the council? Apart from you and I, only the minister, Banomar, and Hosam were aware of my order for the mineral."

"No, I won't," Nayak answered. "But I may have to, if we do not figure this out soon." Then he got up to leave.

Before disappearing outside the door he turned, "And Angla?"

"Yes, sir."

"Do not trust anyone blindly. You may be skilled in fight but you are not well versed with politics yet. You are only a pawn in the grand scheme of things."

14. Piling Worries

"This is disturbing indeed," the minister said. "More so if it was meant for Nigara. The king has been dead for just two days and we haven't yet announced that the prince will be succeeding his father. It's common knowledge that Nigara is being trained for that role."

"Nigara was sent another dish even before the lunch was taken to the visitors' building." Angla told the minister in a small voice, careful of being overheard by the servants cleaning the wide hall in the minister's quarters. They were both standing on the small porch outside the hall, staring at the back wall of the stone temple. "So I am inclined to think that it was meant for the envoy's maid as a kind of warning."

"What else did you find out?"

"No other orders have been placed for the mineral, and Rola confirms that no one was aware of the content of my order, except the four of us who knew about my idea. It is however possible that someone, who has dealt with it on the islands, has blabbed about it to others."

"Do we have any way to find out?"

"I have sent a word to the men there, but I doubt we will find anything."

They were both silent for a while as two servants came to clean the porch. The entire palace was being cleaned and painted for the first time after it was built, thirty years ago. Besides his personal room and an inner office, the minister had a long wide hall in his quarters where he proudly displayed his art collection. He personally discovered, bought, or received each item and had them imported from different kingdoms of Khaga. Each of them was perched in a special place in the hall, where the minister also entertained guests from time to time. Warning the cleaners to be careful with the art, he had stepped out earlier to talk to

Angla. They both waited, as the place was swept and cleaned after the day's painting job. After a while, most of the servants left, leaving only two, a man and a woman, to pick up the scraps and put away the tools.

The minister slowly asked Angla again, "And the king's death?"

"Most of the kitchen staff was absent today morning on account of the dinner yesterday. I could only find out that no large fish or anything of the kind was supplied to the kitchens in the last week."

"And the king's last dinner?"

"He dined with his sister and his brother-in-law. Their son was also expected, but he did not turn up. I was told that he was away from the palace at the time, but no one could tell me where he went. The king's daughter-in-law ate in her own quarters, like she normally does whenever the prince's away. After the dinner, the King went to his quarters—"

There was a loud crash from the hall and they both rushed in to see the minister's ceramic statue of a Kirika dancer shattered to pieces on the floor. The woman servant stood over the toppled stool looking white-faced. Angla observed the minister as he stared at the broken pieces on the floor and reigned in his anger. He knew that the art collection meant a lot to the minister, and nodding to the servant, he bent over to gather the pieces from the floor.

The woman looked at the minister and spoke in a shaking voice, "I am sorry, sir. I was just..."

"Please clean up and leave," the minister told her. He then turned to the other servant and said, "There are a set of large closets in the store room behind my personal room. Please fetch them to my office and set them up against the wall beside the window. Just clean them up and leave."

The man nodded at the minister and left the room. Angla and the minister watched as the woman fetched a broom and swept the pieces onto a wide plate.

"You can come later to clean up the rest, after I put away my collection," the minister told her. "Please inform Mali when you leave." He then turned away and made for his office, motioning Angla to follow.

They walked into the office and waited as the servant brought up the closets, one at a time, into the room. Once he had set them up against a wall as instructed, the servant fetched a broom and a wet cloth to dust and clean the two closets.

The minister still looked disgruntled, so Angla explained, "Mali had to hire inexperienced cleaners because of the heavy work."

"Yes, I am aware of that. I had planned to place all the art pieces safely inside a few days ago. But the king's death and the other plans made me put this away until now."

Once the servant left, the minister picked all the items from their stools, mini stools, shelves, wooden platforms and nails on the walls and placed them carefully inside the closets. After a while, Angla too joined him, careful not to cause another mishap. They worked silently for almost an hour. After they put all the items inside, the minister locked both the closets and slid the keys into a drawer in his desk.

"I am sorry about the delay, but my mind wouldn't have been at peace until they were perfectly safe." The minister told Angla with a small smile.

Angla returned his smile and poured him a glass of water. Then they both grabbed the wooden chairs in front of the desk and sat down.

"I was thinking," Angla started, stirring up their earlier discussion, "that the Second Nation would have also sent someone to oversee the preparations for the Peace Events. They still regard the region of Wisali with animosity, don't they?"

"Yes, they do. If it weren't for the personal discussions with the king and my frequent visits, they would have never agreed to the treaty. But, you are right; they must've already sent someone to Bora because that is where their officials would be staying. Most of them would return almost immediately after the treaty is signed."

"Have you received any news from the Second Palace? I know Irany has been here since the king's death. Kankara must be managing the palace in his stead."

"No, I don't expect to, unless there's any incident. I had sent a note to Kankara on the funeral night with one of my messengers to expect a visit from the Second Nation. I wanted someone in the Second Palace to be alert and aware. I have, however, advised him not to send me any messages, even secretly, lest it looked suspicious to the visitor from the Second Nation."

"Are you now reconsidering your advice?" Angla asked.

"Things happening of late seem to be out of our control. We have only a few days for the Peace Events to start and the situation is delicate because of the king' death. Small incidents could escalate quickly into huge trouble for Jalika. I need to know if any unfortunate incidents, like the one today afternoon with the First Nation's envoy, have happened in Bora. I will, however, have to be careful on noting it in the book. I think there is a spy or spies in our palace."

"And we do not know who they are working for," Angla concluded for him.

15. The Devil's Intent

The Little Brother was still reeling from his meeting with the Devil as he walked towards the warehouse. He had not got a chance to leave a message during the day as the Elder Brother had instructed him to. He was exhausted and he expected at least one of the Brothers to be waiting for him. He quickened his pace as the day faded away.

When he had read the Devil's letter that the guard at the school gave him, he had felt proud of himself. He had gotten at least two things right in his chase of the Devil. The first was questioning the kids about the old man by the lake in the morning. The second was visiting the school with a wild guess that the Devil must have been one of the rogue pickups by the king. He reckoned he must have given the right answers at the school because he was certain that the guard tested him before handing him the Devil's message. The message just told him to meet the Devil by the lake under the tree. He guessed that the old man must be a messenger or a scout for the Devil but he was surprised when the old man turned out to be the Devil in disguise.

"Why the disguise?" he had asked her before parting.

"It has been a few years since I've come here. If Jalika was fast changing when I last left, it has become unrecognizable now," she told him between quick gulps of water. "The King used to arrange things for me before. Unfortunately, he is no longer alive and my previous knowledge of the region has become useless too. Not only necessary for protection, the disguise keeps away unwanted attention. Also, people tend to ignore a poor old man easily." She winked at him at that and he laughed aloud.

As she collected more water from the lake and freshened up, he followed her wordlessly, just listening to her.

"I have other errands to run before I can focus on any unexpected trouble that the King was wary of," she said. "That's where you come in. I need a channel to gather the small but sometimes extremely relevant news and be on the streets without looking suspicious. Then we put things together and see if that tells us anything."

The Little Brother had never met anyone like her. He had met and known women who were powerful or dangerous or both, but she was different from all of them. Those women either were born into a noble lineage and taught to be warriors, or were beautiful and trained to be assassins and spies, or were fierce ones who learnt to survive in harsh ways, or were hunters brought up in wild tribes. But, she seemed to him a combination of all and yet somehow different. He wondered how much of her could he let on to the Brotherhood. Here was a real test to his loyalty. Yet, he knew he would protect her identity, even from his Brothers.

"I belong to the dark and that is where I shall remain," she had said to him. "But my fight is not entirely in the dark and you will become my light if only to provide me a direction, lest I be consumed by the darkness."

When he asked her why she chose him to reveal her identity, she had answered, "You were close to finding out my background anyway, and I'd rather not waste time in these games. If we expect trouble with the Peace Events, then we do not have much time and I need your energy in solving the issues at hand rather than trying to figure me out."

As the Little Brother turned in the big gate and entered the yard, he saw the Elder Brother standing at the door of the warehouse with a lantern in his hand. As he followed the Elder Brother inside, he decided that he would be as honest as possible without giving out anything of significance about the Devil's identity. Once inside, he removed his sack, his food pack, and sat down in the chair opposite to the Elder Brother.

"Long day?" the Elder Brother asked him, "You didn't leave any message here."

"My plan was to come in the evening and talk to you, but I got sidetracked. I received a message from the Devil, when I was investigating one of my hunches, to be at a place at sundown for a meeting in person. And so I went there."

If the Elder Brother noticed the omissions he did not say anything, but he raised his eyebrows in surprise and asked him, “Did he tell why he sought you out?”

“He found out that I was investigating him and so he decided to save us some time. However, he wanted me to keep his identity secret, even from you. He will collaborate with the Brotherhood only if this is agreeable to us, or he will seek help elsewhere.”

“If he was resourceful enough to find about you, why does he need our help?”

“Because the king is no longer present to provide him with what he needs. Since we had a common friend in the king and a common goal in the king’s vision for a safe and protected Jalika, he thought it was the best course to take.”

“Alright, his identity is not an issue with me, though the other Brothers might need a little convincing. I understand the need for secrecy when you have definite disadvantage working in the open. It’s something even the Brotherhood sees the need for. The only person we decided to rely upon is gone.”

“Have you considered approaching anyone else on the council?” The Little Brother asked him.

“There is no one yet powerful enough to keep interference away from us and needful enough to use us without considering us a threat. The minister, as you already know, has his own network of faithful spies and messengers. We don’t know how he would react to our presence.”

“What about the king’s family?”

“I doubt his eldest daughter will be interested in following her father’s footsteps. The younger one is still too young. And the prince, well, has been just a miner so far and never interested in ruling. However, we cannot wait for things to clear for us. The signing of the peace treaty is crucial for Jalika, and it wouldn’t hurt to have more eyes watching.”

The Little Brother nodded. Things have started to get interesting, he thought, satisfied.

16. Becoming a Brother

The Little Brother climbed upstairs to his room with the Elder Brother following. He washed himself while the Elder Brother arranged the light dinner he had packed for the both of them. Then they sat down to eat. The Little Brother thought that it was strangely intimate, like a bond taking life, one he had resisted for a long time.

"I have some news too," the Elder Brother broke the silence. "I received a letter from the Second Brother."

"How could you have received a letter from him already?" the Little Brother asked, "He must have reached only in the morning."

The warehouse and the Elder Brother's house were in a village near the Main Palace, which was on the eastern end of the Wisali. The village was tucked away from the bridge that separated the two regions of Jalika. The Second Brother, who lived and worked as a small officer in the Second Palace, was on the other side of the bridge. The Third Brother, a fisherman, lived closer to the bridge in Wisali region, and the Fourth Brother, a miner who was away on the islands most part of the year, lived in a village almost halfway between the bridge and the warehouse. Communication between the Elder Brother and the Second Brother, even with the other two Brothers helping in between, took at least a day.

"Why are you so shocked? The Second Palace is not a great deal far from the bridge, you know?"

"You are talking about the Evil Merchant's mansion, aren't you, the one that was made the center of all operations in Bora after the war?"

"That was used only for a short while. The mansion belongs to the merchant's family. They all fled Bora after his death, but there was still the risk of them coming back one day and demanding the right to their family mansion. So the council decided to build a new palace in Bora. It is not all that far from the bridge, and there is a direct way from the Main Palace to the Second Palace which would take less than a day on a fast horse."

The Little Brother felt ashamed and a trifle irritated that he did not know much about the developments in the place he belonged to. He had never been to the other side of the bridge and never cared about the region of Bora, but he could have found that out when he was idling away his time the week before.

"But yes, we do have our own ways," the Elder Brother continued as the Little Brother listened with interest. "We explored the region thoroughly and found many lost tracks and abandoned lands that give us a faster route. We even followed the messengers between the palaces. But it wasn't enough. Most messengers use the main road but the urgent messages or the secret ones go through the forests. We suspect that the palace has a network in the tribes to deliver messages quickly using noises or possibly even birds and animals, a practice the Jalikans were not familiar with before the trade with the nations. We are not yet sure how they do that as we never dared to explore that deep into the forests. We tried different ways many times over the years to be sure, and we finally worked out a fast channel that we now use for our communication."

"I guess there are many things that I need to catch up on," the Little Brother said as he waited for the Elder Brother to finish his dinner. Then he got up to put things away.

"We use sealed envelopes," the Elder Brother explained. "The Second Brother only walks till the bridge and leaves the envelope in a secret hiding spot that we change every month. We do not know or trust many people in Bora, and even the region in Wisali where the Third Brother stays. So, he collects the message from the bridge himself."

They both stepped onto the terrace where the cold night greeted them with a light breeze. The Elder Brother continued, "The Third Brother's wife is a trained archer and they live close to a small stream that separates their town from the next village. She shoots the envelope with an arrow to the other side of the lake, onto a tree trunk. It is then picked up by one of the young runners we hired in secret. They get the message through to the Fourth Brother, who then sends it across to me with one of the carts that are on their way to the market."

"Has there ever been any trouble?" the Little Brother asked. He understood why the Brothers did not reveal that information to him till then. He had always acted like an outsider to the Brotherhood, never quite sure whether he belonged. He had never before shown any belief in their faith or any interest in their activities.

"It was tough establishing it. We had to filter out many people before deciding whom to pick as our runners, and they had to be resourceful enough to do it quickly. There hasn't been much trouble since we got everything in place," the Elder Brother answered, watching the Little Brother closely. "We use them only once in a week. But starting yesterday, I told them that we would communicate everyday till the Peace Events."

"So, what was the news?" the Little Brother asked.

"The Second Brother says there is a new guest in the palace at Bora from the Second Nation. It is not anyone whom he recognizes. This person has been given special quarters and dedicated servants. No one is to disturb him and he is given a free reign in the palace."

"Is that unusual?"

"The primary of the Second Palace, Irany, is at the Main Palace. So, the Second Brother doesn't know where the orders came from. However, the treasurer, the king's son-in-law, must have returned today with his wife, so he would soon find out more. Either they received the orders from the Main Palace or the Second Palace has its own secrets."

"That is interesting. I think we need to consider the possibility that trouble can arise from the Second Palace as well. Is it possible that there are rebels trying to divide the regions again or are planning to attack Wisali?"

"Indeed, that would certainly put a new light on the king's death. He had been quite brutal in quelling riots in the region of Bora. I told the Third Brother to be alert about the comings and goings on the bridge and also asked him to monitor all communication between the two regions. We will let the Devil know if we find anything."

The Little Brother nodded, thankful that he didn't have to remind the Elder Brother about supplying their news to the Devil.

"You look tired, go get some rest. Tomorrow, you have to gather some information from people I have marked out in the villages. The Fourth Brother and I will try to gather news from the other islands."

17. Spice and Spies

Riccham Katitaju walked into his room and closed the door swiftly. It was early in the morning and the servants would soon be knocking on his door. After making a note of his findings, a habit he cultivated so that he could be thorough in his daily post, he opened the door to his room and stepped out onto the wide stone porch.

He was housed in one of the many large rooms on the northern end of the Second Palace of Jalika. The palace backyard opened into a building with a small lawn in the center that was surrounded by a wide porch on three sides. It had several large rooms, quite new and unused, and was away from prying eyes, just what Riccham wanted.

It was silent except for the distant palace sounds and the birds chirping in the thick trees surrounding the palace. He rang the bell beside the pillar in front of his room to call for food and cleaning and waited.

He could get used to being served upon, he thought, and he had been in the palace for only a little more than a day. He had been working for his master for only a few months when a message came from the royal court instructing his master to visit Jalika. His master had established a solid trade of spices with many new kingdoms in a few years and had grown in power in the Second Nation. He had many friends in the royal court and often acted as a spy or a negotiator as the need arose. His master was a charming man with many connections and used them well to achieve his means. But a few days before he had to set out for Bora, he fell from a horse and broke his leg. Riccham laughed remembering the incident; his master didn't look so charming then.

When his master realized that he wouldn't be fit to make the journey, he decided to send his young and inexperienced apprentice to do the job in his stead, because he knew that once the royal court turned to someone else for the job, they would not consider him again. He had convinced the royal court that Riccham would be as good as himself in every way. So, Riccham had ended up on his way to Bora with strict instructions from his master.

Riccham had a good education along with physical training. He had learnt as much as he could from his parents who sold spices in the small town where he grew up. Working for a major spice trader was perfect for him, he thought, and if once in a while he had to put in espionage work, where he could use his physical skills, which could gain favors for their trade, there was no harm in doing it.

The Second Nation had been highly suspicious of Bora ever since the unification with Wisali. The Evil Merchant, as the Jalikans called him, was originally from the Second Nation. He established trust and trade without any trouble after he arrived in Bora with his family fifty years ago. But since the destruction of him, his well-established trade, and his well-laid ambitions, the Second Nation had to make a string of tough choices. The Second Nation had also agreed to sign the peace treaty only to prevent advantage to the First Nation.

The Second Nation wanted to be absolutely sure that there wouldn't be any trouble for them in Jalika. In a way, Wisali and Bora were like the First Nation and the Second Nation before the war and the unification. Riccham wondered whether the same would be true of the nations in the coming future. His master told him that there were some officials in the royal court who thought that it was a good chance to ambush the First Nation and its allies. But, the Peace Events were a tradition considered almost sacred by many allies of the Second Nation and causing trouble would certainly break the rules of their alliance. The Peace Events also provided a great opportunity to vie for neutral parties, bring the other allies to their side, and portray domination over the First Nation through friendly games and small performances. But, some recent events had left the great minds at the royal court in deep suspicion of Jalika and the Main Palace's friendship with the First Nation and whether they would arrive in Jalika in a few days with peace or war depended on the findings of Riccham.

Things had worked out well for Riccham so far. He had gained entry at the port immediately after he arrived as the spice trader. He had expected to find trouble in staying at the Second Palace, but the primary had been away when he arrived and Kankara, the in-charge who had dealt with his master many times before, had agreed to provide him with a very private room within the palace and informed others to be helpful to him. As soon as he had settled, he had started enquiring about how things worked in the Second Palace. The cleaning staff and the others had told him that Irany was a council member in the Main Palace and so was a part of all major decisions. Except for reporting the trade and revenue to the council, the Second Palace worked independently, the same as before the unification.

Any information of some importance to Riccham came from a man who was appointed to serve him food. The servant used to work in the Evil Merchant's mansion and was a friend of his master from his previous visits. On continuous prodding, the servant informed Riccham about the secret messages that come from the minister. He also told him that the messages were mostly about security or trade and were sent to different people in the Second Palace. No one knew where or what the message was; the only way was to find an entry in the respective authority's log. A plan formed quickly in Riccham's mind and he asked the servant to help him sneak into Irany's and other officials' offices to see the logs. It took some convincing that there would be no danger of getting caught as both the primary and the treasurer were away, but the servant finally agreed.

Riccham snuck into the treasurer's office and found logs that matched with some of the dates he was interested in. He knew that the treasurer was married to the dead king's daughter. So, it was possible that he had been working for the Main Palace's benefit. Riccham came back to his room and waited till lunchtime the next day. When the servant came the next time, Riccham mentioned doubtfully whether there was any truth to the information about the minister's secret messages. As Riccham expected, the servant was indignant and said that he was sure as he had relatives who worked in the Main Palace and one of them saw the minister send the messages and make entries in the council log book. Riccham then told him that he wanted to see it for himself. Though the servant initially refused, after Riccham parted with a good amount of gold, he agreed to arrange for Riccham to sneak into the Main Palace at night. They agreed that the servant would get Riccham all the details of the visit at breakfast the next morning.

***

In the morning, Ricchám woke up early and snuck into Irany's office. However, he did not find any entries in the log that looked suspicious to him. He returned to his room and waited for the servant to bring his breakfast. He heard footsteps then and stopped his pacing. When he saw the servant walk in through the gap from the backyard of the palace, Riccham smiled. The night would bring his first real adventure. He would sneak into the Main Palace of Jalika and look at the minister's logs. He felt excited, nervous, and overall quite good about himself.

18. Friend in Trouble

The Little Brother was exhausted by the time he reached his room above the warehouse, late in the afternoon. Early in the morning, he had borrowed a horse from one of the local stables and started his visits to the people that the Elder Brother had marked out for him. The Elder Brother did not like riding and hence the task fell to him. Inside his room, he spread a mat on the floor, lied down and stared at the ceiling, knowing that the Elder Brother would arrive shortly to talk to him. After that, he had to leave for an arranged meeting with the Devil.

The Elder Brother had picked three people to talk to. The Little Brother had visited a workman named Shirag first. Shirag worked at a manufacturing unit in Jalika that worked on Bora's trade consignments for the Second Nation. The Little Brother had approached him as someone looking for work and caught him busy with his chores. Before the Little Brother could decide on how to get information from him, Shirag had told the Little Brother that there was heavy work at the unit and they could use any extra hands available. When the Little Brother asked him why there was a sudden surge in the work, Shirag had answered distractedly that the Second Nation had ordered several shipments identical to the ones already dispatched by the unit. Before the Little Brother could press on the matter, Shirag had told him to meet at the unit if he wanted to join work immediately and had left in a hurry.

The Little Brother had then gone to visit a boy who worked in the secondary stable of the Main Palace from where messengers and errand runners borrowed horses with permission from the council members. But the boy, who also taught riding to others, had gone to teach an early morning lesson to a council member's young son. The boy's mother had been reluctant to reveal the council member's name to the Little Brother and had eyed him with suspicion. Disappointed, the Little Brother had left the boy's house.

After a short ride, he had reached the third place and an old lady greeted him at the door. The Elder Brother had already told her that the Little Brother would be coming, but she hadn't expected him so early. So he had talked to her while she cooked breakfast for the both of them. She was a friend of the Elder Brother's mother, and from what the Little Brother understood, she was a friend of most anyone she met.

Her husband had died in the war and she lived alone ever since. The Elder Brother had told him that she worked in the stone temple at the center of the Main Palace. The Little Brother had helped her finish cooking and then laid down the dishes in the small living room where they both sat to eat. She had not asked him why he was there but chatted generally in a delightful manner, describing the temple, its architecture, and how the king had asked the palace to be constructed around it without disturbing a single stone or the large neem tree in front of it. She had told him its history, how it seemed to have a life of its own, and how everyone in the palace adored it. He had listened to it all fascinated, lapping up her words like a hungry cat. He didn't ask her for any information directly, but he had put forth a few questions about the dead king, which she had answered sadly.

In the end, when he bade her farewell and got on his horse, he had thought he hadn't gathered much from her except that the king visited the temple after his dinner every night before retiring to his inner chambers where he read for a short while by the fireplace before sleeping. The king would often speak to her in the morning about his readings from the previous night and she would offer him her opinions. It had been a long ride back to the warehouse. The Little Brother thought the day had gone well for him personally, considering all that he had learnt about the temple. But he was disappointed that he didn't have much information for the Devil. He hoped the other Brothers fared better than him.

After a short while, he heard the iron gate of the warehouse being opened. He waited for the Elder Brother to come up but he didn't hear any steps on the ladder even after a few minutes. So, he got up, splashed some cold water from a wooden container on his face, and stepped out. As he climbed down the ladder, he saw that it was not the Elder Brother who had come, but a lady who was now turning away, probably after finding the warehouse locked. He jumped down the last few steps and she turned to the noise. He recognized her as his friend Katmayo's wife, Nya, whom he had visited the day before.

Surprised to see her there, he strode to her quickly and saw her tired face glistening with sweat as she gave him a worried smile. He motioned her towards the warehouse and opened the door. He offered her a chair by the table and got her a glass of cold water that she accepted thankfully.

"What brings you here? Where is Katmayo?" He asked her as she put down her glass.

"He didn't come home last night. I am worried."

"Did he go on one of his secret errands?"

"Yes, which means he usually comes home by midnight. But he hasn't returned. I sent a word to this man who worked with him for the palace arrangements, but he told me that he hasn't seen Katmayo since yesterday evening. We are new in the village and I do not know anyone there except a few neighbors. I couldn't go looking for him myself given my condition. You said you would be here, so I came to find you."

"That's good. But it's been only a night; maybe he got late finishing the errand."

"But he always sends a word. His work usually takes him to the Chama forest where his parents stay, and he visits them once his errand is done. They came to see us in the village today morning and they haven't heard from him either."

Just then, they heard the gate turn and the Elder Brother walked in. The Little Brother quickly introduced her to him as the wife of Katmayo, whom the Brothers were familiar with and explained the situation to him.

After he finished, she said, "That is not all. Before he left for work yesterday, he found out that a messenger, Raik, who had been sent out two nights before, hasn't returned home. I could tell that it worried Katmayo, but he shrugged it off saying that Raik would soon turn up." Her voice gathered a kind of despair in the tone and the Little Brother could see her frustration in being helpless. "But Raik hasn't been found since."

19. The First Step

The Little Brother promised Nya that they would search for her husband and the Elder Brother arranged for a small wagon for her to go home. After she left, the Little Brother turned to the Elder Brother and confessed to him what he knew about his friend's work.

"I just know that he runs secret errands for the minister. The only thing Nya could tell with confidence about last night's errand was that it was a message to the Second Palace. She guesses that Katmayo usually crossed the Chama forest by himself and then passed the message over to one of the other messengers who then carry it forward."

"This is rather curious," the Elder Brother mused. "A secret message to the Second Palace yesterday night from the minister when Irany, the primary of the Second Palace, is still in the Main Palace. Shouldn't Irany be the one to send any messages, with or without the council's knowledge? What secret business does the minister have in the Second Palace?"

"What about Katmayo? Do you know anything else about the secret messengers? You told me that you followed them from the palace to see how the communication happens."

"I know that most of them use the forests to pass on the messages quickly. We could observe only in the night and we couldn't decipher much in the dark. They usually head straight from the Main Palace to either the Chama forest or the thicket near the graveyard and disappear. Four or five hours later, a messenger arrives at the Second Palace leaving the message for the intended person along with an entry in his log. But do not worry, I will look into this right away and you can join me after your meeting with the Devil."

The Little Brother agreed to meet him at end of the village in two hours and asked, "Was the Second Brother able to find anything about the mysterious visitor?"

"Not yet. I haven't received anything from him today. What did you find out from your visits this morning?"

"Not much. The manufacturing unit allocated for Bora has been working nonstop to fulfill repetitive shipments to the Second Nation. Would you enquire on that?"

The Elder Brother nodded and said, "We haven't had much luck either. There have been no curious incidents on any other islands so far. Lately, there have been many foreigners, even on the small islands. That should be expected I suppose, given the risen popularity of Jalika due to the Peace Events. Who wouldn't want to do business with these resourceful islands, especially with a guarantee of safety with war on the brink?"

"And the Third Brother?" the Little Brother asked.

"He only saw the treasurer of the Second Palace, his wife, and their party cross the bridge yesterday. No one else of any consequence has appeared so far. But I've told him to keep an eye out for anyone strange."

They both spoke for a bit and when the Little Brother realized he was going to be late for his meeting with the Devil, he bade the Elder Brother farewell and hurried away on his horse toward the lake.

***

The Little Brother headed straight for the tree, but there was no one in sight. He got down, tied the horse to the tree, and looked around. Then he heard a movement behind him and turned. The Devil, who was already turning away, gestured him to follow. They went behind the rocks and sat down to eat their lunch. While eating, the Little Brother told her about the news from the Second Brother from the day before, his visit to the manufacturing unit in the morning, and finally the situation about Katmayo that made him late. She listened to him attentively without interrupting and went silent for a while after he finished.

"Does the Second Brother know whether these messages are being received in the Second Palace?" she asked him.

"I thought of that, but he wouldn't know which log to look for unless he knew which person each message was meant for. When they followed the messengers long ago, there were only one or two officials in the Second Palace. But now, there are many."

"From what I know, the king trusted his minister and placed faith in him to run most of the affairs. If my guess is correct, then the message must just be instructions to whoever is in charge of the palace in the absence of their primary. Do you know who that is?"

"Yes, it is Kankara. I will get across a message to the Second Brother asking him to look at his log. But you don't think the minister has some secret agenda? Why else would he use the secret messengers?"

"Maybe he wanted something delivered faster or maybe he was just paranoid, like the king was when he sent for me," she told him.

"Or maybe they weren't from him," the Little Brother said with a sudden thought.

"You are not sure?" she asked him, surprised at his change of tone.

"It was a long time ago when I got the impression that Katmayo worked for the minister. His wife never confirmed or denied it. So I could be wrong."

"Either way, we need confirmation. We need to find out what was in those messages and when they were sent. I think it's time I sneak into the Main Palace."

The Little Brother had expected something like this from her but listening to her telling him casually about sneaking into the Main Palace put him to thought. He was silent for a while as she stepped away to clean. When she returned, she said in a simple tone, "Don't worry. I won't be caught."

"You should probably wear the painted tunic that the servants are wearing in the palace, just in case," he told her and then explained to her what his friend told him about the tunics.

"I wasn't aware of that," she told him, smiling. "Do you have one with you?" she asked and when he nodded to that, she said, "Leave it for me here in the evening."

"I will have to return to the warehouse to fetch it. I will leave the tunic here for you on my way to meet the Elder Brother."

"Alright, I will look into the matter of shipments to the Second Nation at the manufacturing unit in the meantime. If I don't get a message across to you in the night, wait for me here early in the morning tomorrow."

20. What the Records Say

The Devil walked towards the manufacturing unit in quick steps, using the Little Brother's directions that he had given her earlier. She hoped that it would still be lunchtime for whoever maintained the records. Except for a few small places that remained unchanged, Jalika was an unknown territory to her. She didn't know if that was good or bad, but the region had only responded in the best way possible for its survival, much like her. She was proud of the king and she remembered the promise she had made as she stared into his funeral pyre—that she would ensure his legacy continued without trouble. If there was anything that made things easy for her, it was that every office in Jalika kept records religiously. The war had ended in peace and unification, but there was little love lost between the two regions. So, it had been decided that every transaction, every discussion, every message, and every decision would be kept track of, to avoid any miscommunication that could tip over the delicate situation. Thirty years later, even with the unification strong, the tradition was followed with the same vigor.

She reached the small road junction in front of the weapons master's building. As she walked past it, she looked at the house where Banomar's large family lived, without him for most days. She then turned left and headed toward what looked like a dead-end. But she heard voices behind the muddy wall and noticed that there was a narrow lane on the right behind the wall, opening into a large compound. A group of four men was ahead of her, seemingly returning from lunch. As there were loud noises from a distance, she couldn't hear what the men were talking. She made sure they disappeared into the compound and that there was no one behind her, before she entered the narrow lane toward the compound in large strides. She peeked into the compound with her body leaning on the wall of the narrow lane, mindful of any voices behind her and ready to take flight if needed. It was a large compound, with a long road running along its length and buildings on either side of it. The construction was still going on and the loud noises were of the breaking of stones mingled with the forging of metals. The metal work was taking place on the empty space on the left of the road, before the first building on that side. She saw heaps of sand and crushed stones all over.

On the right, there was a small locked room and behind it was a large warehouse. She saw people carrying heavy bags into the warehouse from the workshops in the back of the compound. In front of the room, facing the road was a wooden chair in which an old man sat noting down the return of the workers. The men she saw before surrounded him, blocking his view of the entrance. In a flash, the Devil moved toward the compound wall on the right of the room, straight ahead from the narrow lane, and hid behind two tall wooden ladders.

She moved to the edge of one ladder that leaned against the compound wall and peeked into the room through a half-opened window, but she couldn't see much. The old man was sitting alone outside and the room behind him was locked. She wondered if she could manage to enter the room without the old man realizing. But, one small turn from him and she would be caught. Just then, workers appeared in the narrow lane entering the compound. Behind them came another man, better dressed than the others, with a huge bunch of keys hanging from the leather belt around his waist. The old man noted down the entry of the two workers and nodded at the man with the keys. The man opened the door to the small room with one of his keys, and the old man got up and followed him into the room with his book. He returned a few minutes later empty-handed and headed straight to the narrow lane, which seemed to be the only way in and out of the unit. The Devil noticed him disappear and then contemplated her next move. The workers in the unit all seemed to be in the back, and even the ones moving in and out of the warehouse wouldn't notice her if she moved along the wall. The few people in the front on the other side of the road working on the stones were all turned away from it and did not pose much of a threat. The only problem was the man with the keys, inside the room, who she guessed to be the record keeper of the unit. She considered waiting for him to leave the room, but he seemed to have just returned from his lunch and might not leave soon. Then she looked at the structure of the room and its roof. The roof looked like it was hastily patched together with poor construction. The Devil guessed that it must be a temporary reprieve till the complete construction of the unit finished.

The roof was laid out with a single layer of mud tiles, and dry straw was used to cover gaps and holes. She silently thanked whoever placed the ladders where she stood, as no tree or stone was around to give her an initial lift. She climbed up the ladder closest to the room's wall and inched closer to the roof. She climbed slowly to make sure the ladder had grip on the ground and carefully to not make a sound that would be carried into the room through the open window. Once at the top, she grabbed the edge of the roof and tested her footing. The tiles were laid out firmly and they did not move or creek as she heaved herself onto the roof.

She crawled towards the back end of the roof and found a small hole in the layer of tiles covered with straw. She moved the straw around and adjusted her hand on it instead so that light wouldn't suddenly stream into the room from the hole. She peered through the gap in her fingers and observed the room. It was small, only half the length of the warehouse beside it. It had three wooden desks, one right next to the door, against the wall beside it. Another one was against the wall opposite to the half-opened window and looked unused. A third one lay a little to the back and in the center. Behind the third desk was the man with the keys, and behind him, there was a locked wooden cabinet. There also was an open wooden box beside him on the floor, which seemed to hold record books. One book was open on the desk in front of him in which he was writing while referring to a parchment in his left hand.

The Devil took out a thin, expandable spyglass from her pocket with her left hand and placed it between the fingers on her right hand. She had to wiggle up a bit and lift her head high to peep into the spyglass with one eye closed. With her left hand, she focused the glass on the book and moved it from left to right to decipher the content. The open page had a few entries of the orders received from different kingdoms in the Second Nation and its allies. She could recognize the kingdoms from their symbols drawn on top of each entry. Some entries seemed to be marked with Jalika's seal on a right column, which the Devil assumed meant that the consignment was shipped. But, a few such marked orders were struck off and the exact entries were repeated below. The man seemed to be adding another one to the list, and once he finished the new entry, he struck off an exact marked entry from the top of the page.

The Devil removed the spyglass and put it back in her pocket. She then moved to the edge of the roof again. She lifted herself till her waist and peered at the road behind the narrow lane. She couldn't see any figures moving, so she quickly climbed down using the same ladder and snuck towards the lane along the wall of the compound, mindful of the opened window. Then she made a quick dash, same as before, and walked out of the narrow lane onto the road leading away from the unit.

21. Mystery in Black

The Devil arrived at the rocks by the lake and went to the spot where she had had lunch with the Little Brother. On the rock where she sat earlier, she saw an arrow drawn in white lime pointing to the ground. There was a smaller rock below it under which she found a package containing the tunic, as promised by the Little Brother. There was also a note from him that read:

"The Elder Brother went to the Chama forest to trace Katmayo's movements before he disappeared. The Fourth Brother will investigate the tribes near his village. I shall visit Katmayo's wife and then meet the other messenger's wife as well, to see if they can tell me something more. I will come back here in the night for your note."

The Devil turned over the note, took out the quill and the ink bottle from the Little Brother's package and sat down to write,

"There are no repetitive orders at the unit. Shipments may have gotten damaged or have not reached their destinations for some reason. So, they are working on the same orders again. I think that the visitor at the Second Palace is here to investigate the same. The Second Brother must be well known in the palace, so why don't you go over there and see if you can find anything about the visitor? Be careful when you do."

She left the note under the same stone, took the package, and walked to her place of stay to change and wait for the night.

***

By midnight, she was near the western wall of the palace, between the main gate and the Medica building outside the wall. Normally, someone sneaking into the palace would think to use the fact that the gardens on the northern end of the palace expanded into plantations outside and the wall separating them wouldn't be a big hurdle to cross. But to someone like her, who was well versed with the structure of the palace and its buildings, it was easier to enter the palace through the Medica, which extended on either side of the palace wall. There were several additions to the building outside the wall that she wasn't aware of, but she knew how to traverse from the outer structure to the inner one so she could reach inside the palace wall and into the palace grounds.

Roughly an hour later, she was at the top of the stairs inside the Medica that led to a small back door in the palace grounds. A couple of rooms in the inner building were burning the midnight oil and she took detours to avoid them. She had snitched a small basket with a bundle of gauze and some potions; in case she got noticed entering the palace, she could lie that she was carrying the medicinal basket to someone in the palace on request.

The grounds were well lit, but she used the shadows and the trees to wade her way to the pillared verandah surrounding the palace. She stepped onto the verandah through one of the several openings, near the corridor that would lead to the inner quarters of the minister. She was sure that the minister kept his records in the inner office, rather than in the outer office. She reached the inner palace, dodging the guards and other late-night dwellers, and made straight for the beckoning tree in front of the stone temple. Despite the hurry, she paused for a moment as memories flooded her of the many times she had visited the temple and had sat there with the late king at night. She willed herself to walk around the temple and arrived at the small porch outside the hall in the minister's quarters. The entrance was locked from the inside and it would take her a while to pick the bolt from the outside, even with many years of practice.

Closed doors and locked cabinets always called to her ever since she climbed up a small but daunting hill, leaving her family behind and finding the prince on the other side. Turning her eyes away, she quelled her urge to open the porch door, and moved around the wall toward the front door of the hall. To her surprise, she found the door open and slightly ajar. She knew that the hall held the minister's much prided art collection and she found it suspicious that the door was left open in the night. She looked around to make sure that no one was around and stepped in. To her further surprise, the hall was empty except for a few stools and other furniture that was pushed to one side. The door straight ahead, leading to the inner office, didn't seem to be locked either. She took few steps hesitantly and looked to the door on the left that led to the minister's personal rooms; at least that one was closed.

She walked to the inner office briskly and peeked in. Confirming that it was empty, she stepped in. It was a rather small office with a wide desk in the center, one wooden chair behind it and two in the front. There were two huge wooden closets on one side and a small table and few stools on the other side. There was a small lamp burning on the desk and before she could take a step in that direction, she heard faint sounds of footsteps. She turned left and ducked under the small table by the wall and pulled two stools in front of her as a shield.

She heard multiple footsteps in the hall just then, but only one set entered the office. Through the gaps, she could see that it was a young man dressed completely in black. He was wearing a black tunic, black riding breeches, and black boots. He moved around the desk and slowly moved the chair aside. He worked on the lock in front of him while muttering to himself softly. A few minutes later, the Devil heard a click and then the drawer being slid out of the desk. Then there was silence while he looked for whatever he had come for. She heard him muttering something again and heard the drawer being slid back in. The Devil could only catch a few words, "was right," "days," "proof." He locked the drawer in under a minute and moved the chair back into its position. He then headed to the door, muttering a little loudly, "Send post soon."

The Devil heard his footsteps as he walked across the hall and left through the front door. She waited for a while before she got up from her hiding place and rushed after him. She saw him whispering to someone at the end of the corridor, and then he disappeared behind it. The Devil moved to the side corridor, toward the temple, and waited. She heard someone, whom she guessed to be the person the man in black was talking to, enter the hall in a hurry and lock the inner office. The person then stepped out of the hall and locked the front door. When all was silent again, the Devil moved back to the corridor and headed the way the man in black had disappeared.

She lost him as she stepped out of the inner palace and walked along the long corridors, but then she spotted him again turning into another corridor. He was difficult to spot as he was wearing black, but there was a silver chain around his neck, which shined every now and then under the moonlight. Once outside the palace, she saw him falter. He stopped at a corner, took out a parchment from his breast pocket, and studied it for a while before moving again. She followed him to the edge of the gardens, and when he reached the wall, he climbed a tree and heaved himself onto the wall and rolled out. The Devil climbed up the wall and stayed on it, crouching behind a tree, to see him free his horse outside and ride away on it.

22. Mark of the Royal Court

"You look amused," the Devil said when the Little Brother arrived at their spot, late in the morning.

"And you look worried," he told her, losing his smile.

After leaving the painted tunic for the Devil, the Little Brother had gone to meet Nya, but he hadn't found her home. He had returned as he did not know whom to ask about her whereabouts and found the Devil's reply asking him to go to the Second Palace. He had consulted with the Elder Brother who was on his way to the forest and decided that he should do it. Before leaving, he had left the Devil a note that he would do what she suggested and asked her to meet him late in the morning. The Devil had read the note when she returned from the palace in the night.

"I thought the Brothers wouldn't let you do it," the Devil said when the Little Brother told that he had just returned from the Second Palace.

"The Second Brother didn't want me to. But he was busy with his duties and the visitor was away for some reason. So, I convinced him to let me do it."

"So he was away, was he? What did you find?" she asked without an expression.

"I went to his room directly as the building where he stayed was isolated and no one was around, he told her, excited to share his first escapade. "I did not find anything unusual at first, just a trunk filled with dark clothes, some contracts with traders on the islands, some gold and other jewelry. I went through his entire room twice but I couldn't find anything else. Almost as an afterthought, I checked the washing room, and lo, there was another trunk in the corner beside the door, hiding from plain sight. Its lid was open and at first it looked like it was only filled with used clothes and other sheets. I pushed them aside and started rummaging through it. I almost hurt myself in the process."

"Why, what was in it?" she asked him curiously.

"Well, it was a huge trunk and I knew I wouldn't remember where each thing went if I took out all the contents. So, I put both my hands in to feel its contents. There was a bow and a wide tube with arrows in it, the tips of them pointing out. I could see a small wooden box beside the bow and went for it. While taking the box out, I accidently touched one of the arrows. The bloody thing sprung open like a spitting viper and split itself into three sharp thin blades, almost slicing my hand in the process."

"Split arrows," the Devil's expression grew sharp. "They are a mark of the royal court of the Second Nation. That means, he was trained there and must have been sent by them."

"Most definitely. I found letters in the box that had snippets of information along with a few instructions. I quickly skimmed through them. He was told to find out if someone in Jalika was interfering with the trade between the Second Palace in Bora and the Second Nation and its allies. There was information about shipment arrivals and a few names of the people involved."

"So, my guess about him is correct. Some shipments have definitely missed reaching the kingdoms and they are now suspicious. But why would they send an untrained spy?" the Devil wondered.

"Why do you say that? You just confirmed that he was trained at the royal court."

"Yes. He might be well equipped in physical skills, but he's a terrible spy."

"How do you know that?" the Little Brother asked, his eyes narrowing as he looked at the Devil with interest.

"I saw him at the Main Palace. While you were raiding his room, he was going through the minister's records. But the entire time he was in the minister's inner office, he was muttering to himself and was careless. He had some inside help, someone who opened the doors for him, but he didn't try to keep his voice down or his steps light. He looked young and was most definitely not trained for the work."

"Why do you think he was there?" the Little Brother asked her.

"To verify the minister's messages, which I am now sure went to the

Second Palace. He must have looked at the dates and the subjects of the messages. He also muttered about sending out a post; it must be to whoever sent him here for this job."

"How did he know about the secret messages in the first place? And who helped him get into the Main Palace unnoticed?"

"The secret messages are not really a secret," the Devil explained. "At least to those who work closely with the officials; anyone could have easily told him. We need to find out who was helping him; he couldn't have made friends so quickly in both the palaces."

"Should we track him and find out who he is dealing with?"

"Definitely. Let the Second Brother take care of that in the Second Palace," she said and turned away, looking thoughtful. "What we need is a little help in the Main Palace."

"Whom do you have in mind?" he asked her.

"Do you suspect the minister still?" she asked curiously.

"It doesn't align well with the knowledge that I have of him. If he is indeed a culprit, he is not doing a good job of it," the Little Brother answered honestly.

"Yes, I think we should take a chance by approaching the minister," she sighed and looked away.

"How do we approach him and how do we convince him about what we know?" the Little Brother asked her, noticing her change of expression.

"I know just the right person for that, but he might not be ready to help me."

The Little Brother raised his eyebrows but didn't say anything.

She continued, "But we need proof; the minister needs to know that we are telling him the truth about the incidents. So, we need a plan to catch the attackers of the messengers."

"The Brothers can take care of that. Two of them will wait in the forest and when the minister sends out a message, you give a signal to me so that I can follow the messenger. The Brothers will join me once we reach the forest. But, with the Second Brother out in Bora, we are of course only four members, and may not be enough to overpower a large group."

"You shouldn't do that anyway," the Devil told him. "If the enemy finds out about us, it will alarm them and lead to unstoppable actions.

Maybe you should pose as night travelers, plan your moves to stop the attack, and capture at least one attacker for questioning. But before that, we need the minister's next messenger working with us."

"What do you plan to do?" he asked her

"Someone in the palace is definitely working with the enemy and my aim will be to find out who that is. But, I cannot do that from the outside. So today, I will have to pay an old friend a visit. If I convince him, he will provide us a way to approach the minister. I may have to let him know about the Brotherhood as well."

"I will send out a note to the Second Brother about keeping an eye on the visitor. The other Brothers will be at the warehouse today afternoon and we shall discuss the plan. When do we meet again?"

"We shall meet at sundown." She remained silent for a while and then said in a decisive tone, "I will not reveal everything to my friend immediately. If he doesn't agree with me, he may try to stop me, in which case, you should still work out the plan. We do not have the time to convince him to help."

23. Trouble in the Command

Angla walked towards the chief's office, trying hard to keep the waves of despair in his mind at bay. His life was in a frenzy keeping up with his regular duties, preparation for the Peace Events, and investigating the king's death and the poisoning incident. He had been running around the palace like a headless chicken and now he was going to report to his chief that there was no progress in proving his innocence in the attack on the envoy. He arrived at the small inner hall that led up to the outer offices, thinking that he could catch up with the minister first before going to his chief's office. It was a good thing his chief's office was upstairs; he would probably prosecute Angla if he saw him still meeting the minister alone despite his well-veiled warnings. The truth was that Angla trusted no one. He had developed a deep friendship with the minister and had gained the trust of his chief when he became his Second, but he never took anything for granted. He knew that in the worst of situations, self-preservation trumps everything else and so he never extended too many expectations to anyone in his life. He was not a cynic, just a well-prepared man. He always kept an eye on things, carefully watched people, and listened in on conversations. Yet, somehow, he had missed an evil plot brewing right under his nose.

He took the three steps leading to the door on the right and saw that neither the minister nor his assistant was present in the minister's outer office. Sighing, he turned to the window by the assistant's desk and took out his pipe. He could easily guess that someone powerful was behind the poisoning incident; the person seemed to be well informed about everything. Certainly someone from the council or one of their confidants was involved, either voluntarily or involuntarily. Angla never jumped into anything without thorough analysis, but this time, he neither had the time nor the complete information to understand the situation. He put out his pipe and walked into the hall again. As he made his way to the stairs leading up to his chief's office, he heard his chief's loud voice drifting down the opened door.

"Another one! How could this have happened? I told you to be extremely careful."

"I oversaw every step myself," someone answered the chief and Angla recognized him to be Chandraj, who helped Kaliki in handling Jalika's trade.

"We didn't decide the date of the shipment till one day prior. We loaded the material at night and used different workers instead of the regular ones, without telling them what they were carrying. I personally informed you, the minister, and the prince about the delivery here in the Main Palace. Kaliki informed Irany in person as well."

The chief was silent for a while, and then he said, "I know there is no fleet of large ships leaving from Jalika, but what few ones we use for trade are all new and look the same. How could they have known which one was leaving with the shipments? Could it be because of our routes?"

"Our routes vary depending on the destination, and we do not know the route followed by the purchasing nation once their people take over the shipment. All the attacks happened after the ships left our territory. After the handover, most of our crew leaves the deck immediately to return to Jalika in smaller boats. Only a select few travel till the destination to finish the transaction and return with the ship, but they are always kept in the dark about the route. I handpicked them carefully; there is no way someone could've known about the routes beforehand."

"Well, that the attacks happened outside our territory is the only reason the Second Nation hasn't attacked us already. This incident, I have to report to the council since it's the third largest shipment that was lost to the bandits in just a few weeks."

"The newly converted unit in Wisali and the older one in Bora are both working at full capacity."

There was silence again and Angla climbed up a few steps to listen to his chief speak. He heard Nayak saying, "So far, the attacks have been on insignificant shipments and were not too big a trade loss for the kingdoms. But one more such attack and they could suspend trade with Jalika. I shall write a personal advice to the nations about changing routes and increasing security to the ships. You take care of safe delivery from our side."

Angla did not wait to hear the rest of their conversation, sensing that it was coming to an end. He dashed down the few steps that he climbed up and ran silently towards the minister's office. There he waited to listen to Chandraj's footsteps. After a few minutes, he heard him climb down the stairs and leave the hall. As a second to the chief, he knew the other seconds well. Chandraj was picked by Kaliki from under a trade manager in Bora and was made responsible for trade of the Second Palace. Angla waited for another few minutes before making his way again to the chief's office.

He knocked on the half-open door and entered after Nayak answered.

"You look busy. Do you want me to come back later?" Angla asked.

"No, no. I was about to send for you. Tell me, were you able to find something?" Nayak asked, motioning Angla to sit.

"Not much, sir," Angla answered honestly. "I went to the kitchens with the maid. No one seemed to know who placed the dish on the tray, and the maid herself could not remember whom she spoke to. The newly hired people for the kitchens seemed to have started early because of the funeral dinner, and since it was done in a hurry, no proper records were kept."

"And the theft of the poison, any progress on that front?"

"It's not as well kept a secret as we thought it was. Since it was toxic and needed to be carefully handled, everyone from the miners who worked on it on the islands to the people who carried it to the workshop was told about it."

The chief sighed and said, "And since many had access to the workshop, we cannot identify who entered without authority. Well, keep looking. We need answers. The questions are only piling up."

A dark cloud came over Nayak's face and he looked all of his forty-five years, which prompted Angla to ask, "Was there any other trouble, sir?"

Nayak looked bleakly at Angla and answered hesitantly, "No, just everything seems to show how unprepared we are to deal with the unexpected."

Angla knew that the chief was talking about the king. The king had single-handedly managed to turn a group of a few towns and villages into a kingdom that was worth the notice to the rest of Khaga. He was the only common confidante of all the council members, and in his absence, everyone was wary of the others.

"We'll find our way through. We just have to make sure the Peace Events go fine without a hitch," Angla spoke softly, which brought Nayak out of his reverie.

"Of course, don't mind me. I am just tired from skipping meals," he said in an even voice. Then he pointed to the paper on which he was writing and said, "The crowning of the prince is to be in three days, just a day before the Peace Events. It will be a small event, but we have much to do."

24. Run Out of Luck

After planning the arrangements for the crowning ceremony with Nayak and adjusting work among the people already in place for the Peace Events, Angla headed to the kitchens for a meal. He did not speak to anyone there, unlike the morning when he questioned about the poisoning and the King's last dinner. He had hit dead ends on both pursuits. He did not yet know if the king's death was a murder, and he did not have any answers about the poison either. There was, however, one remaining lead that could reveal some answers, and he decided to pursue it before meeting the minister. He also had to decide whether to bring up the issue of missing shipments with the minister; he did not want to reveal that he eavesdropped on his chief's conversation. If he waited, the minister would learn about it in the next council meeting. Either way, there was nothing for him to do in that matter. It was an unspoken rule that no one should interfere in the matters of the Second Palace unless asked to.

After his meal, Angla headed to the garrison to leave instructions about the security arrangements for the crowning ceremony. He then made his way to the visitors' rooms inside the palace, where the king's nephew was staying on his visit with his parents. Angla did not know him; the only reason he was interested was because the nephew had missed the king's last dinner without a reason. Angla racked his brains for his name but couldn't recollect it. The king's sister and her husband still lived in a remote village where the king grew up as a child. They had never visited the palace before, but only accepted the king's personal invitation so that the king's brother-in-law, who was sick, could consult the healers at the Medica.

As Angla turned into the small gravel yard separating the inner palace from the visitors' rooms, he saw the king's nephew leave his room. Deciding to check his room later, Angla followed him silently. The nephew headed to the stables and Angla noticed him speak to one of the minders about borrowing a horse. He looked much older than Angla remembered from his visit to the king's village. There was a bounce to his walk, but he lacked posture. He reminded Angla of a wild rabbit, excited and scared at the same time. Angla too walked up to the stables and asked the minder whether the nephew borrowed a horse on the night of the king's death. The minder told Angla that he did let the nephew borrow a horse that night and one or two times after that and asked if there was some trouble. Angla told him there was no trouble, but asked him to keep an eye on who borrowed horses. He then untied his regular horse and rode through the west gate of the palace after the nephew who headed toward the market.

The nephew turned left, without entering the market, and rode into the empty road that led past the market and the first village after that. After crossing three villages, the nephew slowed down and led his horse toward the hills marking the end of the third village. It was almost halfway to the king's birth village and Angla started to worry that the nephew was just headed home.

The nephew rode along the narrow ledge by the hills and reached the other side. Angla waited for a while before following the same path. There was a large plantation of mango trees on the other side and the narrow road curved left before the plantation's fence. Angla got down, tied his horse to a tree by the fence, and walked along the road. Behind the hills, covered by the plantation on the other three sides, was a large compound full of wild grass and large trees. The nephew's horse was tied to the first large tree and there was no sight of him. In a distance, he could see several tree houses skillfully balanced on a few old, strong trees. Most of them seemed to be occupied by groups of people. Angla could see two other horses and a bullock cart under the shade by the hills.

Angla approached the nearest tree house that looked empty. He climbed up the wooden ladder and peered through the windows. He could see two men sleeping on the floor. He walked in and checked to find that they were inebriated. He looked around and found out exactly where he was—a gambling den. He could see the game tables and boxes filled with claims. The claims were mostly for trinkets, or furniture, or bags of grain. By one look of the place, it was clear that the operation was run by amateurs. From where he was standing, Angla could peer at the window of the next tree house, where the nephew was seated at a table with several other men. Without a word, Angla climbed down and walked back towards his horse.

Worried about the new problem, and frustrated at the time wasted, he jumped on his horse. He rode fast and returned to the palace in an hour. He returned the horse to the stables and went to his small office near the main entrance of the palace, a place he used only as a drop point of messages for him that he checked once or twice a day. There were two notes for him, one from Banomar about an increment of supply to the patrol guards and one from the minister informing him that there was a council meeting after lunchtime and that Angla should meet him after that. Angla took the note from Banomar and left the room. On his way, he stopped to speak to the man in-charge of the patrol guards about the weapons. Angla also informed him about the gambling den that he had walked into earlier and told him to meet later to discuss the problem. By the time he reached his secret spot, the council meeting was already in progress and he could hear Kaliki's high pitched voice float up to him.

"Now that we all agreed about the plans for the crowning ceremony, I have one issue to bring forth. We've had a few bandit attacks on our shipments to the Second Nation. There is no cause for alarm yet, they are happening beyond our territory, but it may affect our trade. Irany, Nayak, and I will be taking care of the situation so it won't come to that."

"Alright, let us know about the progress and ask for any help you need," the prince said in his even tone. "We do not want anything to antagonize the nations now. Speaking of which, has there been any more news on the unfortunate incident with the envoy?"

"Not yet, I've put Angla on it but he hasn't been able to uncover much," Nayak answered the prince.

"That is alarming," Vihoro said. "I cannot stall them longer without any progress."

"I think it would be best if we throw it out in the open," Nayak said in an urging voice, which made Angla think that the chief had already said this before, maybe the first council meeting of that day in the morning, which Angla missed.

"No, that would result in chaos and the word would spread quickly to the Second Nation that they are suspected in a poison attack," the minister said.

"You are guessing at that. We need more ground to work on . . ." Nayak started in a high voice, but the prince cut him off when he heard other murmurs. Angla now pressed his ear tightly against the roof, shielding his face from the wind.

"Let us not make hasty decisions," the prince said. "Chief, if you are already burdened, would you like the minister deal with . . . If until the crowning ceremony, we do not . . . then we shall do what you suggest."

There was further discussion with opinions from the Rahugmana, Banomar, as well as Irany, but Angla could only hear it in bits due to the heavy wind. Realizing that this would go on for a while and that either the minister or the chief would inform him of the decision, he got down and headed to his quarters. He was still sweaty from the ride and the wind on the roof only exaggerated the sticky feeling on his skin. He took a change of clothes from the small rope tied outside in the backyard of his quarters and headed to the cleaning rooms. When he came back from a quick bath, fresh and clean, he found an unexpected visitor in his room.

25. The Plan

The Little Brother opened his eyes and groaned. His head felt like a rock and he closed his eyes immediately in pain. He opened them again slowly and looked around. He was in a small room with clean white walls, a small window, and a closed door. Except for his bed and a small table beside it, the room did not have any other furniture. He could see through the window that it was dark outside. Inside the room, there was a long candle burning on a holder on the floor between the table's wooden legs, throwing a dull light over the room.

He had been brought to the Medica, he remembered, with a broken arm, a sprained ankle, and a mild injury to the back of his head. He felt the bandage around his head with his good arm and closed his eyes again in pain. He had been given some potion to dull the pain and help him fall asleep, but evidently it was not enough. It must be early hours in the morning and he couldn't believe that only about four hours ago, he was arguing to go out to the forest as the minister's secret messenger.

***

The Devil had approached Angla, the second in command of Jalika's security, about the recent events. The Little Brother did not know how the Devil was friends with Angla or why she hadn't approached him first instead of the Brotherhood. Angla listened to everything she had to say but refused to let the minister get involved without proof. He had, however, agreed to their plan of following the messenger and capturing the attackers in the act. Angla had already known that the minister was to send a message to the Second Palace that evening about the crowning of the prince, and he convinced the minister to hand over the responsibility of conveying the message to him. How he did that was another question to ponder over for the Little Brother.

It was an uncertain plan and they did not have time to smoothen out the rough ends. First, they didn't know how the attackers knew when the messenger left the palace. Second, since they weren't about to use one of the regular messengers, they weren't sure if the attackers would even make an appearance that night. Then, they had to decide who the messenger would be and who would stop the attack. The minister did not use female messengers and Angla couldn't be involved, being well known. That left only the Little Brother, and he voluntarily agreed to do the job.

It seemed simple enough to him at the time. Take the message from the minister's inner office when he would be busy elsewhere, borrow a horse from the stables, and head straight to the Chama forest while the Devil kept an eye out on him to see if he was being followed. Then Angla would follow him discretely till the forest, where the Little Brother would go to the stream, place the message in a wooden floater, and send it down the stream. If he was attacked at any time, he should shout for help and the other Brothers, hiding at a safe distance from the stream, would come to rescue.

Angla had raised the security in the inner palace with two groups of his trainees after his talk with the Devil. They were told to observe and inform only him; as far as others were concerned, they were running errands for the many arrangements. Both the Devil and the Little Brother were given a clearance with them. Utilizing the free reign given and her knowledge of the palace, the Devil identified strategic positions for them and scoped the palace with the help of a young leader from one of the trainee groups, the only one to meet her in person. Meanwhile, the Little Brother introduced Angla to the Brotherhood and they exchanged their notes on the passage of the secret messages. Finally, a few hours from sundown, it was time to implement their plan.

Just like he was instructed, the Little Brother handed over a note from Angla to a minder in the stables and asked him to ready a horse. He then walked to the minister's office, which was empty. He simply pocketed the note on the desk and walked out. He did not meet anyone else on his way in or out, except for the workers moving about, but he knew that the Devil was watching him from somewhere. He got on his horse and rode along the shortcut from the palace to the forest that Angla had drawn for him on a map. He was tensed and apprehensive, like a person without swimming skills about to jump in water. But, he remembered that Angla was following him closely and that the Brothers would be waiting in the forest. He increased his pace till he reached the forest and carefully directed the horse on the unfamiliar ground toward the stream, where the night light was warm and shining.

He tied his horse to a nearby tree and waited to detect any movement as his eyes skimmed through the area. Nothing caught his attention in the dark and it was eerily silent. He walked towards the nearest pepper tree and took down one of the wooden floaters stocked under a branch. He wrapped the note from his pocket in two thick, wide leaves and tied them along with a small stone. He placed the assortment in the floater and took it to the stream.

He placed the floater in the water and directed it downstream with a thin stick. He observed it till it disappeared and threw the stick away. Just when he was about to get up from his squatting position, he heard movement behind him and all other thoughts rushed out of his mind. He fell sideways and rolled away, missing the club aimed at his head by inches. He turned and saw three men dressed in black, all ready to attack. When the one closer to him raised his club again, the Little Brother pushed at the rock behind him and jumped to the other side. A single thought made its way into his brain—call for help. But even as his vocal cords shouted with all their strength, one attacker tried to get hold of him while the club made its way toward his head a third time. He could successfully fend off the one trying to catch him, but he wasn't so lucky with the club, and it hit him at the back of his head. The attacker closest to him caught him in the middle as he fell.

As the pain blinded his eyes, and his mind went numb, he heard footsteps of the Brothers running and their shouts of alarm. The grip of the enemy tightened for a moment but he let go to rush after his colleagues who were already escaping from the place. In a moment of inspiration, the Little Brother turned and caught hold of the enemy's leg, but with his eyes still half closed and no coherency in his limbs, he tripped on a root and fell, taking the enemy down with him. Fallen and now hurt in his ankle, he still managed to hold on to the enemy. But the enemy found a stone and hit him on the knuckles with it. As the Little Brother loosened his grip, the enemy got up to run away, only to meet the Elder Brother, who had finally arrived. The Fourth Brother rushed after the others but he came back disappointed as they had disappeared into the dark. As the enemy struggled with the Elder Brother, the Little Brother knelt by a stone, blood streaming from his arm. The enemy jerked his head violently, throwing out kicks at the Elder Brother with his legs. He freed his one arm and pulled at the thread around his neck. When the thread broke free, he swallowed the small pasty cloth at its end, and within seconds dropped dead in the Elder Brother's arms.

***

The Little Brother shuddered in his bed in the small Medica room. He had never seen anyone die before and it turned his blood cold just as it turned the enemy's body blue with poison in minutes. Sighing, he opened his eyes and stared at the ceiling. After a while, he turned and saw a container of medicine on the table beside the bed. Slowly, trying not to exert pressure on his broken arm, he lifted himself up a little. There was a small note with instructions to drink the medicine when in pain. He took the container with his good arm and drank from it. He also drank water from a glass, which was kept on the table, to keep down the bitter taste of the potion, and fell back on his bed. Then he looked out of the window and watched as the palace came alive in the glory of the morning light.

26. Into the Palace

The Little Brother did not remember falling asleep, but when he woke up again in a few hours, he felt much better. The bandages around his head and his arm itched, and he had an urgent need to relieve himself. His headache was only mild, but his hand was throbbing badly. He lifted himself up carefully and pushed himself into a sitting position. He put his feet gingerly on the ground and noticed the dry cloth tightly wound around his ankle. He put pressure on the sprained ankle and sighed in relief when it was just uncomfortable, not painful. Thanking the gods that at least his legs were fully functional, he stood from his bed and walked to the door. Just then, the door was opened by a middle-aged woman, who looked pleasantly surprised to find him out of his bed.

"I just came to see if you were up," she said, and without waiting for a response from him, called for someone outside. A thin, young man, probably a few years younger than the Little Brother, came running. She told him to direct the Little Brother to the cleaning rooms and assist him if needed. Gently refusing his support, the Little Brother motioned him to show him the way.

When he was back a few minutes later, the woman had already changed the sheet on his bed, filled the glass with water, removed the candle, and was sweeping the room. He waited for her to finish and leave, and then went in and sat on his bed.

She came back a few minutes later with new bandages and more medicine. She removed the cloth around his ankle, asked him to move it around, and then left it like that when he told her there was no pain. But soon he was wincing as she removed the bandage around his arm, applied medicine, and wrapped it in a new bandage. She then changed the one around his head and left, instructing him to sound the small bell on the table if he required anything. Once the door closed behind her, he leaned against the wall and thought about what to do. But his door opened again, and the Devil entered the room silently.

"You look much better than yesterday. How are the injuries?"

"The arm is throbbing and I have a mild headache. But why are you here so early? You came all the way from your place to check on me?"

She raised her eyebrows at his disbelieving tone and said, "I never left the palace." She sat down on the floor beside his bed and recreated his pose by leaning against the wall.

"Right, so what happened last night? Was anyone following me as I left the palace?"

"I did not notice anyone in particular. I think it was one of the servants; there was no one else around."

"How are we going to find out who it was?" he asked her.

"I have decided to stay in the palace. It is where everything seems to be originating from. Angla has cleared us anyway with his people, and I'll continue to pose as a servant to move about freely." There was a wicked smile on her face now as she continued, "Angla is with the minister, convincing him that that would be the best idea. I'd love to hear that conversation."

Quelling the urge to ask her about her relationship with Angla, he asked her another question that came to his mind, "The minister knows everything now?"

"Yes, pretty much. We proved that his messengers were being attacked. He cannot pull in the records from the Second Palace without causing alarm, but he will soon send notes to the Second Brother to verify the records. And there have been other incidents as well. Our suspicions about the missing shipments were true and there was a poisoning incident with the First Nation's envoy staying in the palace."

"So what is the minister planning to do now?" he asked her. "Surely, he would want to discuss all these matters with the prince and the council?"

"I doubt he would. He already suspects that the king's death was not natural and that someone in the palace is responsible," the Devil answered.

There was anger in her voice then and the Little Brother again wondered about her connection with the dead king.

"Angla has already been investigating the matters on his own. The council only knows about the poisoning incident and they had decided that the minister should handle it. I think he would continue to do that, and if he believes us to be his allies, he'll take our help. He already met with the Elder Brother."

"None of them were badly hurt, were they?" he asked her worriedly.

"No, but I think they now realize that the trainings they went through on their own are not enough to handle such situations, something even the minister pointed out. For now, they will continue to be our eyes and ears on the streets, while Angla and I work from inside the palace."

And what would he do, he wanted to ask, but remained silent lest she told him to simply rest while they took care of the matters. There was a moment's silence while she looked at him and he avoided her eyes.

"And just like before, you will be our channel between them and us," she told him.

"What do you mean?"

"Your room, right here, would be our rendezvous. The Brothers would scrape through Jalika for the bandits and leave with you any information they find. Meanwhile, you are to gather information on everyone in the Main Palace and piece it together. Good thing your leg feels alright and you can move around without anyone's help."

"The bandits," he said, remembering his attackers, "they're the ones behind all of this?"

"We do not know if they're actually behind this, but they certainly seem to be everywhere," she told him. "Angla too rushed into the forest to get to you when he heard your shout, and the attacker whom you managed to hold on to swallowed the arsenic from the thread around his neck when he saw Angla. You see, they have done this before. Black clothes, attacks in the dark, swallowing poison to avoid capture—that's how they operate."

"And the escaped ones?" he asked her.

"They were gone before Angla came, so they do not know yet that he is aware of them. The Brothers left the dead bandit in the forest. So if they return for him, something that I doubt will happen, they will think that the travelers who came to your rescue just moved on after helping you. The message you sent got delivered to the Second Palace successfully. We received a return message from the Second Brother.

Angla sent a reply asking the Second Brother to tail the visitor from the Second Nation in case the bandits plan to harm him in any way. Evidently, they were behind the attacks on the shipments as well. They attacked the ships after they left our territory."

"Who are these people? A week ago, I'd never even heard of them. And now they seem to be involved in all the problems here."

"I can answer that for you, son," the minister said, as he walked in from the open door.

The Little Brother gave a small jerk in fright, but the Devil sat unmoved. Angla was behind the minister looking at the Devil. They both entered the room and Angla shut the door behind them.

27. For a Better World

"Angla told me what happened last night. How are you feeling now?" the minister asked the Little Brother, approaching his bed.

"Better now, sir, just a painful arm."

"It was brave what you did. Though the Brotherhood is not essentially trained, I can see why the king would have wanted you to remain as you were. As we all found out, we need people like you on the streets of Jalika." The minister then turned to the Devil, who was staring outside the window. He walked toward the window and stood against the light. When she looked up, he asked her, "You are ready to investigate discreetly in the palace posing as a servant?"

"Yes," she answered.

"Good, anyone else from the guard, even posing as a servant, would easily be recognized. You need to be careful though; there are people in the palace that might still recognize you."

All the while Angla stood silently by the door looking at the Devil curiously. He then turned to the Little Brother and nodded, "You must of course know already that we would be using your room as a meeting place for all of us. It's a private room in a deserted corridor, so no one will bother us here."

"For now, we gather information," the minister said in a grave tone. "No one is to make a move without discussing with the others. You may be brave but sometimes one cannot predict what dangers lay ahead. And when it comes to that, we may need all arms we can get."

"The bandits," the Devil asked, looking at the minister, "what do you know about them?"

"It's a cult started by a man named Hrudrak. He propagated the idea that the world of Khaga has been created by the wrong gods as an experiment and so was filled with evil minds and suffering bodies. He believed that there was another perfect world out there and we only need to free ourselves from this one to reach the new world."

"Freedom in death?" the Devil queried mildly.

"Yes, that was his motto," the minister answered. "He was a great orator and he would gather people to give speeches. He wrote books and songs about his propaganda. They spread slowly and he gained popularity. His devotees started springing up everywhere, in mysterious situations, motivating people to commit suicide. In many cases, it was later found that people had been killed or forced to commit suicide.

"The First Nation banned the group, their leader, and his teachings. Soon, the Second Nation followed suit, when they found out that children and young people were being murdered in the cult families. There was a hunt for their leader but he was never found. His close group of disciples were caught and imprisoned, but no one knew if the leader was even dead or alive. However, he had several other devoted followers who vowed to carry on without him. Their aim is to end this world and then kill themselves.

"Several years ago, a few of their members approached our king for shelter, but he refused. Just like in the other kingdoms, practicing or preaching the cult has been banned in Jalika, and anyone found doing that would be imprisoned. But it never came to that. After the king's refusal, they disappeared and there hadn't been any news for quite some time. But somehow they grew in power and strength. About five or six years ago, there had been several incidents in both the nations by the cult, and people came to refer to them as 'the bandits'. But they stopped as abruptly as they had started. And it is only recently that they are surfacing again."

There was silence after the minister finished. Then the Little Brother spoke, "They attacked the ships, maybe to provide themselves with supplies. Could it be that they're planning to launch an attack during the Peace Events?" He suddenly thought about the causalities that would result from such an attack, with both Jalikans and the visitors attending in large numbers, and shuddered.

"That could be a plan, but that would require a huge strength in numbers," Angla answered. "If they are not already here, they would need ships large enough to carry them just in time. Our shipments were not using such ships."

"They certainly seem to hold a grudge against Jalika," the minister said, turning away from the window to face the room. "They seem to have connections in high places, and not just in our courts, since they could figure out the trade routes of the Second Nation. And if indeed they are responsible for the king's death, then we are in even more trouble than we imagined."

He then turned to the Devil and asked, "Even as one of the servants with a free reign in the palace, how do you plan to find out anything? We cannot afford to lose any more time. The crowning ceremony is in two days and the Peace Events a day after that."

"I have already questioned all the people even remotely involved in both the incidents in the palace and I do not have any further information," Angla added, staring at the Devil's face.

The Devil was silent for a while and then turned to the minister, "The visitor from the Second Nation was pointed specifically to your messages by someone. I think whoever is planning this is trying to place the blame on you. If my guess is true, then the envoy from the First Nation could also be getting such hints or clues that could lead him to you. I will keep an eye out on his communication and follow his every move. Sooner or later, he should get desperate enough to break his word with Nayak and take matters into his own hands, if he hasn't done that already."

Angla continued to look at the Devil and said, "You said he was wearing all black that night when he snuck into the minister's office, but you also said you didn't see anything else to indicate that he was one of the bandits. If what you say about the bandits pointing him to the minister is true, then he might have had contact with one of them."

Angla now turned to the minister and suggested, "In that case, maybe we should more than just keep an eye on the visitor in the Second Palace. If we approach him honestly, we may be able to convince him to reveal the information he has and the sources for it."

"Alright, travel there immediately but do so without drawing attention," the minister told Angla. "And you cannot disappear for long from here, so make sure you return as soon as you have anything. And if the visitor doesn't agree, leave him alone, but set people on him round day and night. We do not want him to come to any harm from the bandits but neither do we want him to send any panicked letters to the royal court."

After that, Angla took their leave and left for the Second Palace, and the minister asked the Devil to accompany him back to the palace. But before leaving, he remembered something, and turned to the Little Brother.

"The corridor next to you leads to the rooms in private use by some members of the council. There is a historian in one of the rooms with a bad heart, but his mind might interest you when you do not have anything to do here." He smiled kindly at the Little Brother and walked out the door.

The Devil winked at the Little Brother and said, "Your breakfast is on its way." Then she too turned and left, leaving the room silent once again. After a few minutes, the old woman from earlier walked in with a food tray.

28. The Cinnabar Cause

After a quick meal with the minister, the Devil changed into worker's clothes in the cleaning rooms of the servant quarters. She then walked towards the stables near the visitors buildings outside the Main Palace and eyed the house where the envoy was boarded. The minister told her that the envoy had requested for an office and had been provided with a small room on the ground floor of the same building.

As she watched, the envoy came out of his office. He approached the soldier, sitting beside a pillar outside, whom, for all her alertness, the Devil did not notice until then. The envoy moved out with the soldier who showed him the way to some place in the eastern end of the palace. Both of them looked in that direction intently, and the Devil found her gap to run to the back of the building. She knew that the ground floor had a huge hall and three small rooms, one of which was being used as an office by the envoy. The other two were not furnished and so were just locked at the moment. She picked the lock on the back door of the hall and entered the house. She approached the office room and listened before turning the lock on the door of the room. She pushed the door in slowly and when she entered, she faced a wooden desk and a chair behind it that the envoy used. She noticed that there was a window on the other side of the room with a view of the palace. She ducked out of sight of the window and walked to the middle of the room.

There was a fireplace on the wall, beside the door from which the Devil had entered, and a small fire was burning. In Jalika, the nights are usually cold, but at that time of the day, the sun had already come up and it was beginning to get hot. Wondering why the envoy needed a fire then, she squatted down to observe it. She saw that between the logs, slowly burning in a blue flame, was a parchment. With a small log, she prodded so it fell out of the fire. With no choice but to use her bare hands, she put out the fire using her sleeve, careful not to let the cloth catch it. The parchment had already torched in the fire and was delicate to her touch. So, she let it remain on the floor and bent low to decipher the words on it.

It looked like a letter and she couldn't see who it was from as the fire had burnt that part away. From the rest, she could decipher that it suggested that the king was poisoned. One word in the middle caught her attention and she bent too low, almost touching the parchment with her nose, to read it. It was not clear at first but after racking her brains for similar looking words, she concluded that the word was "cinnabar." Carefully, she turned over the parchment to see if there was a mark on the back. When a seal gets punched onto the envelope carrying a letter, in most cases, it leaves an imprint on the letter, and she could see from the faint lines on the back that the letter came from someone high in the First Nation's court.

The Devil gathered the burnt pieces of the parchment and threw them back in the fire. She then wiped the floor without a blemish. After that, she walked to the desk and saw that there was no drawer there. She then searched the room for other hidden places, but did not find any. So, she left the room, locking it back, and left the hall the same way she had come. She crept her way toward the stables and walked briskly to the palace. The office rooms, the new halls, the outer corridor running around the palace were constructed recently, and the Devil was not familiar with them. As she did not know where the outer office of the minister was, she walked into the inner palace and towards his chambers. Just as she turned into the corridor leading to the hall outside the minister's inner office, she saw the envoy leave it and cross paths with her. The minister was standing at the entrance and looked surprised to see her there. She looked at him expectantly and he motioned her to enter. They both went into the inner office and he closed the door. He motioned her to sit and went to his own chair. He picked a beautifully crafted vase that was on his desk and moved his fingers on it delicately. The Devil noticed that the handle on one side looked only half-made and asked, "Was it crafted like that?"

"No, it's broken, as I just discovered. It would need careful mending. I might've to do it myself; you don't find many craftsmen here privy to the details of working with cinnabar."

"Cinnabar!" she exclaimed in a sharp tone, and he looked up from the vase. She looked at the vase intently now and asked, "It's a mineral isn't it? Is it mined here?"

"No, I got it from the court of Queen Leona of Bumlin when I was touring the kingdoms of the Second Nation. Merin, the envoy from the First Nation, was quite interested in the piece."

"Why was he here?" she asked him.

"He heard about my art collection and came to see it. I told him that it was shelved for a few days because of the activities going on and the people moving in and out. I suggested he see it later once I arrange it back, and maybe bring his wife with him as well. But he insisted on getting a quick look first. He also commented that it shouldn't be shelved during the Peace Events, but displayed proudly to the visitors. It was all rather odd. Why do you ask?"

"I found a burnt parchment in his office fireplace. It had information on the king's death from a high official of the First Nation. It suggested poisoning and I also found the word 'cinnabar' mentioned. I recognized it as a mineral and came over here to ask you about it."

"About the king's death?" the minister looked thoughtful. "The letter can't have come from that far; it has only been a few days. That must mean it was from someone already travelling here for the Peace Events. Did you say cinnabar? And you mentioned poison; that must mean they suspect that the king was poisoned with cinnabar."

The minister now stood up from his chair and frowned deeply. After a minute, he said in a low voice, "They would have to heat the cinnabar and make sure the king breathed in those vapors."

"That must be why the envoy was here," the Devil guessed. "The second half of the letter, which I couldn't read, must have directed him to your collection and the broken handle here on the vase must've confirmed it for him."

"So far, we had thought that it was something he ate and Angla focused only on the last dinner." The minister looked at the Devil now and said, "You need to trace the king's movements on his last day and figure out how it was done. Those poisonous vapors would have affected him quickly, depending of course on the dose. And no one else even remotely displayed such symptoms. So, concentrate only on the second half of his last day; especially when he was alone."

He was silent for a while and the Devil simply observed him. Then he said, “But how would anyone know about all this? The only one let near the body other than the family was Vaidyana and she had only consulted with Hosam. I need to speak to them both.”

He turned to her again and said, “Talk to the servants and see what you can find out. To think that I provided the poison for the king’s death!” He exclaimed with a fierce look on his face. But he quickly calmed down and said, “I need to be careful though, if people already doubt that I poisoned the king, then interrogating the council members would only make matters worse for me.”

“Alright,” the Devil stood up. “You could start with Hosam as he is the only one, other than you, who possessed knowledge about these minerals. I’ll head to the Medica later and see if I can get any information about who handled the king’s body till its cremation.”

29. Smoke and Fire

After leaving the minister's hall, the Devil walked around the temple and approached the king's quarters. Like the minister, the king too had a hall for meeting large groups, an inner office, and his personal space. While the minister's personal space consisted of a bedroom, a work room, and a wide open area, the king's personal space consisted of a bedroom, a small library, a sitting room, and a garden. The garden started from the open space beside the tree in front of the temple and wound around his hall toward the back of his private room. The library and the sitting room were on the other side of the hall.

Even though the garden was tended to, the rooms in the king's quarters were all locked and left empty after his death. The Devil did not want to sneak into those rooms as they had all been already cleaned and cleared. In the morning, she enquired a maid in the cleaning rooms and found that the king had hired a squire three years ago to assist him when he broke his hand in a small accident. The boy was being trained in the Medica when the king came in looking for a healer. When he told the king that he lived too far from the palace and was looking for work in order to stay in the palace, the king had offered him the position of his squire. The Devil decided to talk to the boy and while she was in the Medica, find out if the Little Brother had any news for her.

On her way to the Medica, the Devil saw two women walking towards the palace. One of them, she guessed was the envoy's wife as her clothing was different from the attire typical of the Jalikan women. The other woman, the Devil presumed to be the prince's wife. The Devil had never seen her before, but among all the royals that she had set her eyes upon, no one looked a better fit than her. Even from a distance, the Devil could recognize something unreal about her; unfocused eyes, sharp features, still face, and surprisingly pale skin. But clad in a rich green sari with her long black hair framing one half of her face, and the bright jewelry shining on her ears, neck, and hands, the prince's wife twinkled like a star under the bright sun. The Devil could only stare as she disappeared into the palace. Suddenly remembering her mission, the Devil continued toward the Medica.

The Devil reached the floor where the Little Brother was stationed and approached the woman who took care of the patients on that floor. On asking her about the king's squire, she was told that he had just gone for his meals and would be returning in a short while to stack up the potions. The Devil requested the woman to send the boy to the Little Brother's room once he returned. Then she walked to the Little Brother's room and knocked. She entered the room and found him standing by the window, staring at the palace.

"Admiring the view?" she asked him, walking to his side.

"Yes, but not aesthetically. I have just heard hours of history of the establishment and of the king's rule. I can't help but wonder at how much struggle this palace withstood in just a few years."

"And no doubt, there is more to come," the Devil commented. "So, you met the sick historian that the minister mentioned?"

"Yes, sick only in health. He is as sharp as the both of us. I've asked the Elder Brother to get me my journal and some ink the next time he visits so that I can put it all down. Apart from the history lesson, I did gather information on everyone important in Jalika."

"Were the Brothers able to find anything?" she asked him, noticing his satisfied gleam about the history he had learnt.

"Looks like the bandits have spread well in Jalika. We are beginning to see a pattern. It started with the smallest of the islands and spread stealthily to Bora and Wisali. It has been so far restricted to the villages and not the towns; that would've put them under the palace's attention. I think the palace needs to look at the villages more carefully than the towns."

"Are there any connections leading to the palace?" she asked him.

"A few," the Little Brother answered. "Nayak's brother-in-law, a smithy in the market, has appeared in a few of their meetings that have recently started in Wisali. But Nayak does not keep in touch with his wife's family, so we do not yet know if he is connected."

The Little Brother walked to his bed and sat down. "I have started to identify all the people that are either important or are well connected to someone important. The Brothers can keep an eye on their movements outside the palace."

"Good, any word from Angla or the Second Brother?" asked the Devil, still standing by the window.

"Not yet. What about you? Were you able to find anything?"

"The envoy got a letter from an unknown First Nation official that the king's death was due to cinnabar poisoning. There is a cinnabar vase in the minister's collection that has a broken piece missing and now the envoy suspects him."

"What?" the Little Brother whipped his head around to her. "Someone stole a cinnabar piece from the minister's collection and used it to kill the king so the blame would fall on the minister. My word, that's slick."

"Yes," the Devil agreed. "I came to the Medica to talk to the king's squire about his last hours and where he could've inhaled the poisonous vapors. Since no one else was affected, I am inclined to think that it was done in his personal room where no one else was allowed. But you have been there when the Brotherhood met the king. What can you tell me about the fireplace there?"

The Little Brother shook his head to recover and answered her, "When we looked in from his garden, he was reading by the fireplace and the old lady who works in the temple told me that that was his routine before going to bed. When I was in the room, the only thing I noticed was that the room was rather small for a king. There was just a bed, a small opening leading to the cleaning room, a couple of closets, a long table, and a small reading table laid out on a mat by the fireplace. The fireplace in itself was nothing unusual, just a small shelf in the wall with logs of wood burning mildly and a shutter to pull down and cover the shelf."

"A shutter?" the Devil considered. "That would have prevented the king from seeing if there was anything other than logs burning there. But he always cleaned his room and maintained everything in it himself. Who could have gone in and how did they get in?"

"What did the minister say to all this?" the Little Brother asked her.

"As far as the general population is concerned, the king's death was natural. So, he is looking into how someone outside Jalika could have gotten all this information to have sent a letter to the envoy. The network of bandits seems to be much wider and deeper than we thought. He went to talk to Hosam and then he would talk to Vaidyana. But I do not think they would know much."

Both of them were lost in their trail of thoughts till they heard a knock on the door, which the Devil moved to open. A small dark boy entered, carrying a tray with food for the both of them.

30. Servant Shenanigans

As the Devil made her way to the new smithy, where she was told that she would find the palace's cleaning in-charge Mali, several thoughts whirred in her head. Quizzing the king's squire had thrown some light on how someone could have poisoned the king. The boy spoke freely but he was still in disbelief that the king was really gone. He told them that he only helped the king with his medicines, carried his messages around the palace, and accompanied him on his outings. He was not a squire in the regular sense as the king was self-sufficient and did not want someone to tend to him at all times. When she asked him about the king's last day, the boy said that there was nothing particularly unusual. The king had been in the council meeting all morning. After lunch, he had a discussion with Vihoro. Then he went into his office to make notes and spent the entire evening there, sending out letters. Late in the evening, he had met with his sister and her husband and together they left for dinner, and that's when the boy had also retired to his quarters. He did not see the king again.

The Devil then asked the boy to describe the king's quarters to her, not the layout but the arrangement. He told her that the hall was brightly lit with long windows and had heavy furniture; it could fit as many as fifty guests. The library and the sitting room were small, with wooden shelves full of books and a few chairs. The boy had only been to the king's inner room once to help him when his hand was hurting. Otherwise, the king was strict about not letting anyone inside his room. The king cleaned his room early in the morning and locked it while leaving, taking the only key with him. He retired to it only after dinner, and in the meantime, it was kept locked.

That Devil had never visited the king in his room. She either met him by the temple or by the gardens outside the inner palace. But from what she found out from the Little Brother and the squire, she couldn't see any way other than using the fireplace in the room to poison the king. Moreover, the king read by the fire every night after retiring to his room and then promptly went to bed without any outside contact. So she asked the squire about the fireplace in particular, how it was stocked and whether there were any incidents concerning it.

She and the Little Brother remained silent as the boy thought hard, and then he slowly said, "Yes, now I am certain it was on his last day because the cleaning had started only three days prior to that and they were clearing the hall and the corridors. The servants usually leave the wood for his fire in the hall, just outside his room, and the king picked it up himself. But that evening, one of the cleaners found the logs still lying there, and went inside to place them in the fireplace. The king was in the cleaning room and didn't see it happen. But waiting outside his office, I did, and informed Mali immediately. When she asked, the cleaner said that he didn't realize that the room was out of bounds. She quickly dismissed the servant and told me that she would apologize to the king."

So, the Devil came to the smithy to talk to Mali about the incident and also inquire the whereabouts of the servant who tampered with the king's fireplace. The smithy inside the inner palace was newly built and Mali was working with a few servants to clear up the material the construction crew left, while the smiths, who had already been working there for a few weeks, waited for the noise and the dust to clear out. The Devil stepped into the small lawn in front of the smithy and waited. The lawn was square shaped and in the middle of the corridor connecting all sides. On one side, opposite to the smithy, was a wide arch that led to a large inner garden and a well furnished yard, which was used for the king's family events. The Devil stood with her back to the arch, facing the entrance to the smithy, which was earlier just a store room. On her right were a wall and a small opening leading to the outer palace and on her left were the quarters of the prince and his wife.

As she waited, the Devil saw a line of five workers carrying metal boxes from the workshop to the hall in the prince's quarters. They looked like toys, she mused, all with grim faces, wearing the same tunics, and carrying those boxes in a similar fashion. Everyone around her was wearing the painted tunics, mostly in white, with a small colorful painting of some portion of the palace. She smiled to herself, imagining what the visitors would think of them.

Just then, Mali stepped out of the smithy and the Devil walked toward her. Before stepping out of the lawn, the Devil let the workers, who were now leaving the prince's quarters, walk past her. The Devil carried with her a letter from the minister, and she showed that to Mali when she refused to talk to her. Mali was in a hurry and so told that she could spare only a few minutes. She told the Devil that she remembered the incident where a cleaner had entered the king's room but she had immediately made him leave and had apologized to the king personally. She didn't remember who the servant was; it was one of the many new people she had hired. She then turned and left without giving the Devil a chance to put forth further questions.

While the Devil debated what to do next, a woman came out of the smithy and placed a metal box in her hands, ordering her to take the remaining stuff from the smithy to the store room in the hall in the prince's quarters. No choice but to obey, the Devil entered the workshop and started gathering a few pieces of metal work lying on the slab where the smiths were working. The woman closed a cupboard door and walked out of the smithy, with a glare at the Devil. Cursing her worker's attire, the Devil took the box and walked toward the prince's quarters.

There were three store rooms on either side of the lawn. Of the two smaller ones, one was transformed into a smithy. The other one was adjacent to it, but its door was inside the hall of the prince's quarters. The large store room, to which the Devil headed, was between the yard and the lawn on the other side of the smithy, and also had its entrance from inside the hall. Though the hall was part of the prince's quarters, it was used for common purpose. It was wide and bare, with a total of six doors, two of which were to the store rooms on either side of the entrance door. The door opposite to the entrance lead to a small verandah, the one on its left lead to the gardens and the one on its right lead to the couple's rooms.

By then, everyone working outside had left and it was eerily silent. But as she stepped out of the store room, the Devil heard footsteps, and she peeped out to see one of the servants coming out of the other store room, on the right side of the hall. He was adjusting his tunic, like he had put it on in a hurry, and was walking out of the hall. The Devil recognized him as one of the five workers who had come in earlier and she realized that she had seen only four men leave when she gave them way. The man who just left was the fifth one and he had changed his tunic for some reason. It was noticeable because the new one had less of white and more of the color on the back. Then as she turned her eyes away from him towards the store room, the Devil thought she saw a woman leave the room. As she stepped out into the hall, the woman disappeared into the prince's quarters. The Devil mused that the worker was having an affair with one of the maids, and deciding not to dwell on it, she left the hall.

31. Questions and Connections

A little later, as the Devil walked out of the inner palace and toward the Medica, she saw the same palace worker again; the one she had seen coming out of the storeroom with a changed tunic earlier. This time, he was walking hastily on the road toward the main gate. She saw him open the small door beside the main gate, which the palace workers used, and walk out of it. He disappeared quickly, without a nod or a look in the direction of the guard posted there.

Looking at him leave, the Devil realized how easy it was, in the current situation, to get into the palace as a worker. After all, she was doing the same thing. She wondered if that man was really a worker, or whether he came to just see the maid. If the latter were true, why would they risk doing it in the palace, right outside the prince's quarters, even if it were in a storeroom; they could've gone somewhere else. He seemed to be in a hurry both times the Devil saw him. Was the meeting planned or did they just happen to meet there when he was put to work in the smithy?

Despite her decision to not dwell on the affair that she had stumbled upon, the Devil couldn't stop the questions from bursting into her mind. Why did he change into a different tunic? Could he have just picked up another tunic lying in the room? Why would there be other tunics in the storeroom? Could the maid have given him another tunic? Why would she do that? Was there really enough time for the two of them to have done anything? The Devil saw him coming out of the smithy only a few minutes prior to that. And the Devil did not see the maid adjusting her clothing. If it wasn't an affair, could he have gone there to just talk to her and then changed into a different tunic? If so, then why? A sudden thought struck the Devil and stopped her in her tracks.

She looked around the palace and saw workers, all dressed in the painted tunics, moving about with their duties. Amid them were guards here and there, all in their long reddish brown tunics, thick black belts, and loose white trousers. However, they were too few in presence, and most were rooted to their spots. It was the palace workers who had a free reign. She thought about the incidents so far—the poisoning of the king and the envoy's maid, the visitor from the Second Nation sneaking into the minister's quarters, attacks on the messengers, and the business with the shipments. All of them could have been done by the workers, effective and without a trace considering the many newly hired people, all wearing similar tunics.

The Devil looked down at her own tunic and saw the busy streets of the main market painted in vivid colors. She saw the tunic of a servant passing by and saw the stone temple of the palace painted in detail there. That's the key, she concluded. That was probably how information was being passed among the enemy circles without direct contact. She jumped from her spot and almost ran to the Medica to talk to the Little Brother.

She found him on his bed, scribbling rapidly in a small bound book, which he put aside when she walked in. She quickly brought him up to speed on her thoughts and then asked his help to be her lookout as she searched the palace. The Little Brother quickly got down and fetched his boots. He prepared himself as the Devil continued to talk, with a little animation and a tinge of self-derision.

"We looked at all the incidents in isolation," she told him, as they walked out. "We found the involvement of the bandits and assumed that someone important inside the palace was helping them with the information. But, we did not stop to think about how that information was being passed along or how the incidents kept happening, seemingly without a trace of the perpetrator. It's the palace workers and they are using these blasted tunics."

"Ah, simple and brilliant!" called out the Little Brother.

"We start with the storeroom where I saw that man change tunics earlier," she told him. "I don't remember seeing any clothes in the maid's hand as she left. So we might find the discarded tunics there."

"What maid?" he asked her. "You saw someone leaving from there?"

"Yes, sorry, I did not mention that before. I initially thought it was an affair, but I discarded the idea later. I forgot to mention her completely when I spoke to you."

"Who was she? Did you get a look at her face? How old did she look?"

"I only saw her back. And she definitely must be the princess's maid because she was not wearing the palace uniform of long white tunic, but a simple off-white sari. Why, what do you know?"

"Well, remember I told you that the Elder Brother had many contacts both inside and outside the palace, most of them simple people like daily workers? He gathered as much information as he could about the connections with the bandits and let me know when he came to visit me earlier. Among the few people in the palace that seem to be connected to the bandits, one is the princess' maid. I did not enquire further as I thought that we should be looking at only the important people. I mean, even if she was conspiring with them, she wouldn't have much power, would she? The princess is not a part of the council and the prince only became one recently?"

"We'll decide that later," the Devil said as she directed him toward the inner palace and straight to the storeroom in the prince's quarters. They looked around to make sure no one was nearby and opened the lock. It was dark and the Little Brother and the Devil went to light each lantern hanging on either side of the door on the wall by a nail. Softly closing the door, they turned back to focus on the room as the lanterns threw light on all corners. It was a small room and there was hardly any space to move. The only narrow strip of space was from the door to the opposite wall, in the middle of the room. There were boxes, bags, closets, and trunks on either side, some locked, some half open, and some so old that they were covered in dust and spider webs. The metal boxes, which she had seen being brought in before, were kept in order on the right side of the door, one on top of the other. The Little Brother and the Devil each picked a side and started searching deeply. They opened the locks, threw aside the doors, and dug deep into each box. Finally, after a few minutes of heavy, sweaty searching, the Devil found a straw bag, pushed deep between two old trunks by the wall, underneath a broken wooden table. She fished it out and found that it was stuffed with tunics. The Little Brother stopped his search and came to stand by her. She took out the tunics from the bag and threw them on the floor in the middle of the room. As she spread each tunic, the Little Brother took out his notebook and his quill, focused sharply on the tunic closest to him and started to make notes.

32. A Devil of a Day

The Little Brother left the storeroom first as he had agreed to meet the Elder Brother outside the Medica at sundown. The Devil remained behind to give the whole storeroom another sweep, after which she put everything back in place before locking it up. Once that was done, she stepped out into the hall. The surroundings were empty but she heard low voices. They were coming from across the hall, from the yard outside. She walked toward the window by the door but stopped a little distance from it when she heard the voices again. It was the prince, she recognized instantly; he was talking in his calm, placating voice, just like he used to do with her.

The Devil hesitated, but then slowly took a few steps toward the open window and peeped through it. It was getting dark, but she could clearly see the three figures sitting in the middle of the yard around a wooden table. The prince's wife and his youngest sister were with him and they seemed to be having the evening tea together. Yes, he was fond of his tea, the prince, the Devil thought. She had to move away before anyone spotted her, but the Devil stood there fascinated, watching the prince deep in conversation with his sister, who was listening to him attentively. Taking a deep breath, the Devil looked away from him, bringing forth the resistance that she had developed over the years. She focused on the prince's wife who was sitting on the right, a little apart from the other two and quietly sipping her tea. She was a perfect work of art, the Devil thought. The lady was hardly moving, and her eyes were focused on the tea pot on the table; she didn't seem to be even listening to the conversation. Finally, when the Devil was about to turn, the prince's wife moved to put her cup down and looked at the other two. They barely noticed her, engrossed as they were in their discussion. She continued to look at them, back in her unmoving stance. Shaking off her reverie, the Devil grudgingly turned away from the window. Without looking at the prince again, she walked away.

The Devil went to the Medica and found the Little Brother in his room. He launched into a speech as soon as she closed the door behind her.

"I queried the Elder Brother about the maid and he says there is definitely something to dig deeper there. She was once the only assistant to the late queen. She was with the queen until her death shortly after moving into the palace. No one knows if it was just the queen's death or if something else had happened, but the maid turned into a totally different person soon after." The Devil moved into the room and placed the Little Brother's book on his bed. Then she pulled a stool from the corner of the room toward the bed and sat down.

The Little Brother continued, "She left her husband and her son and went to live in her parent's old hut alone. She never worked again until four years ago when she started working for the palace again, this time in the capacity of the prince's wife's maid."

"How did that happen?" queried the Devil.

"All the Elder Brother could find out was that she was invited to the prince's wedding, and soon after that, she was working in the palace. All the people that the Elder Brother spoke to were eager to tell on her; she seems to be a sort of terror to the other women working in the inner palace. She is the only one who talks to the princess and is very possessive of her position. Ever since the smiths were hired and the jewelry smithy was established, the princess has been busy, and the maid has been behaving like hell on fire with everyone."

"What's her name?" the Devil asked

"Her name's Sanita. The Elder Brother had never heard of her before yesterday."

"Me neither," the Devil said. "Does she have any connection to the princess?"

"Not that we know of," the Little Brother answered.

"What's the princess' name?" the Devil fired her next question.

The Little Brother looked at her with raised eyebrows and said, "Mudrika." When she remained silent, he said, "The Elder Brother is going to enquire into the maid's life thoroughly. Nayak doesn't seem to have any connection whatsoever with his brother-in-law other than the casual family gatherings that happen once in a while. So at present, the maid is the Elder Brother's only lead."

"Alright, we should do some digging of our own in the palace," the Devil finally said. "But, we have other things to work on first. Let's get on with them."

The Little Brother opened his book, and one by one, they both carefully looked at the drawings and the notes the Little Brother had made from the paintings and the seemingly random scribbling on the discarded tunics. The Little Brother put them on wider papers and they both tried to understand what they meant. They took a break after an hour to get some food but got back to work immediately. As they worked, the Devil became more distant and more silent, while the Little Brother became more excited and agitated. And when Angla walked in two hours later, he found them with wild eyes and strained necks, with papers strewn all around them.

Angla had a small injury on his forehead and several scratches all over his body, and it was clear that he had rushed to the room in a hurry. The Little Brother and the Devil looked up at him questioningly.

"The visitor from the Second Nation is badly hurt. We had to bring him here in an emergency. He's still unconscious." As soon as he finished saying those words, Angla collapsed on the bed. The Little Brother and the Devil immediately moved into action. As the Little Brother rushed to get medicine, the Devil sprinkled Angla's face with water and wiped it with a cloth. Then she applied the medicine that the Little Brother got and tied a bandage around his head. All the while, he simply lay on the bed with his eyes closed. Once the medicine was administered, he opened his eyes slowly and sat up.

"Were the Brothers with you?" the Little Brother asked.

"Yes, three of them," Angla answered. "They are not badly hurt. The Second Brother remained in the Second Palace, while the Third and the Fourth Brothers rode here with me. They took some medicine and left after putting the visitor in the next room."

He pointed to the wall on the right and continued, "I've asked two medics to tend to him. They are with him now."

"What happened?" asked the Devil, clearing out the papers so Angla could lean back on the bed.

33. A Shocking Surprise

"I met the Brothers on the bridge, and we all went to the Second Palace together," Angla started his story. "The Second Brother directed me towards the building where the visitor was staying, and I went there alone as the Brothers waited a few paces away from its entrance."

The Little Brother and the Devil were sitting on either side of the bed where Angla was reclining and they could hear movements and noises from the next room where the visitor was being treated. He had fallen unconscious on the way and the medics had just informed Angla that he was still that way.

"I found the visitor in his room and approached him as an emissary sent by the minister," Angla continued. "But that turned out to be mistake because he panicked and asked me to leave right away. It took me a while to convince him that I didn't mean any harm to him. He did calm down eventually, but he did not believe me when I told him that he was being set up. In fact, he was ready with a long letter to be posted to his master, stating that the minister and the First Palace were influencing the Second Palace in a wrong way and were plotting against the Second Nation. I asked him to reconsider his facts and promised him proofs if he could give me some time. But before he could respond to that, a servant came in to talk to the visitor, and he jumped up in fright as he recognized me. He ran out of the room immediately and took off before I could detain him. I asked the visitor about that servant and that's when the truth came out, every stinking bit of it. The servant was the one passing information to the visitor since the beginning, and it was him who helped the visitor sneak into the minister's office. How a mere servant could have arranged that in the First Palace is not clear to me."

At this, the Little Brother and the Devil looked at each other, but remained silent. Angla noticed them and paused. But the Devil shook her head and asked him to continue.

"Anyway, the servant had run off and the visitor was telling me how he snuck into the palace. All of a sudden, there was commotion outside the room and I rushed to the door. I saw a group of bandits there and they launched into an attack as soon as they saw me. There were at least ten of them, and I had to stand inside the door so that I could deal with only a few at a time. The Brothers came running, and seeing that the bandits were trying to get to him, the visitor too joined the fight. He was a good fellow; he knew his tricks, and he kept fielding the blows well. The bandits were fighting to kill and we had to use all our strength to fend them off. The five of us were winning over them, but then the servant came running and went straight at the visitor, hitting him with a log. Caught unaware, the visitor took a few blows before I could draw the servant back. In the fight, I killed the servant and two of the bandits, while the Brothers killed six. The visitor killed one, and the remaining two killed themselves as we injured them badly.

"None of us could recognize who they were. We do not know whether the servant panicked and brought forth his backup or if it was a planned attack. We also do not know whether they meant to kill the visitor and make him disappear or kidnap him and keep him under their guard. Either way, whoever sent them there would soon guess that something was amiss. So, while we tended to each others' injuries and disposed of the bodies, we hatched up a story at the Second Palace that the visitor was invited over to the Main Palace and that I had gone there to personally escort him here. Then we packed all his stuff, loaded them into a cart, and set here immediately. At first, he seemed alright, but he grew weak as we rode and lost consciousness soon after that. We brought him straight to the Medica and dumped his stuff in one of the empty buildings in the street nearby. I posted a guard there informing him that a visitor from the Second Nation would be staying there."

Angla paused for a while and then said, "It will be a tragedy to lose the fellow. Fortunately for us, he hadn't yet posted his letter to the Second Nation."

"But what if he doesn't regain consciousness soon?" the Little Brother asked. "Whoever sent him here would expect updates soon and grow suspicious as time passes without a letter."

"Well, we keep an eye on him for now, and once he regains consciousness, we try and convince him that it was the bandits plotting against him, not us," Angla answered. "If he doesn't listen, then we make sure that he remains silent till the Peace Events. If he doesn't wake up, then we may have to send a letter ourselves somehow. The letters he received and the one he wrote would give us enough clues."

They could still hear movements from the next room and sounds of the door being opened and closed constantly. Then Angla looked at the book and the papers that were kept aside and asked them what was going on. Realizing that the Devil was not talking, the Little Brother told Angla about their day crisply. As the Little Brother talked, Angla's face broke tiredness and grew alert.

"It's an effective means to communicate, given the current situation in the palace," Angla commented. "And if people like the princess' maid who knew the place well were involved, then it's possible that all the incidents were implemented just by the servants without any involvement from a higher official."

Throwing a glance at the Devil, whose face did not show any expression, the Little Brother said, "That seems possible, but from what we deciphered of the drawings, we suspect that the plans came from someone in the council, because there is a lot of information. There are drawings of the king's personal room, his garden, notes about his habits and routine, and there are drawings of the cinnabar vase in the minister's collection, among other information. Some of the scribbling that we haven't deciphered yet seems to be about the shipments that were attacked."

Angla glanced at the Devil now and said, "Not every member of the council is privy to all that you mention. Even the few, who are meant to know, would be informed mostly after the shipment has left our port. And often, these dealings do not happen in the Main Palace. So someone could be passing this information from outside the palace. Looking at their network, it seems they have spies everywhere."

"The king, and after his death the prince, would have been informed of everything that's going on in the palace," the Devil mentioned slowly.

"So, what are you saying?" asked Angla, looking at her with narrowed eyes.

"I can see one common connection to all the people involved," the Devil answered Angla, and then she went on to say a name that shocked him, "Mudrika."

34. Suspicion and Stake

The night shifted outside the window and the palace lights blazed their brightest. Looking at them, the Little Brother moved to pour oil in the lantern inside the room and raise its flame. Everything was silent; the movements in the next room stopped as well. A medic came in and informed Angla that they were done attending the visitor. The patient had opened his eyes briefly, but as they had given him some potions, he fell asleep immediately. The medic advised them to keep an eye on him through the night and said that he would return early in the morning. If the medic thought it odd that the three of them were together in a medical room in the night, he didn't show it. After Angla thanked him, he nodded and left, closing the door after him.

When it was silent again, Angla looked at the Devil and she spoke, "I think the prince's wife is involved. Hell, she could've planned the whole thing." Angla was about to say something but the Devil continued, "She used to have at least one meal with the king everyday where they must've discussed matters of the palace, and since the king's death, the prince has been with her. They may be her source of information and the maid is her connection to the bandits."

"You are unbelievable," Angla said in an incredulous tone, and it was the first time the Little Brother saw him in anything but his calm demeanor. It was also the first time he spoke to the Devil in anything but an indifferent tone.

"This is not about him," the Devil told Angla and glared at him.

"Of course it's about him. When has it ever been anything but him?" Angla shook his head, and when the Devil opened her mouth again, he simply continued in a tight voice, "The first memory I have of us doing something together is you dragging me across miles of fields, barefoot, under scorching sun, with bleeding knees that hurt because we jumped down a tall wall, realization weighing on our minds that we would get in trouble with our warden later, just so you could get a single brief look at him from afar."

The Little Brother drew in a breath. For a minute, it looked like the Devil would erupt with anger but she looked at Angla calmly and asked, "Who suggested these painted tunics for the palace workers?"

Angla's face stilled and he looked at her for a long while before he asked, "How do you suppose she planned all this? She barely speaks to anyone; it's a well-known fact in the palace. The king and the prince are the only people she interacts with. And do you think that in those small conversations, they somehow managed to tell her all the happenings in the palace so she could hatch this plan? How do you suppose this maid of hers convinced her to support the bandits and plan these incidents to wreak havoc in Jalika? And what would she achieve by doing all this?"

"Why don't we find that out? We do not have any leads now other than the maid anyway," the Devil answered him.

"Alright, fine," Angla said, and turned away from her. "Tomorrow I shall track down this maid and talk to her."

The room fell silent again. The Little Brother looked at Angla's stiff back and said, "You should go take rest. We shall continue to decipher these scribbling and drawings and let you know if we find anything."

Angla didn't move for a while, then he turned and looked at the Devil, "I am not going to the prince and accuse his wife of being a traitor and neither will the minister."

The Devil just looked at him while he continued.

"The minister told me that the envoy had informed him in the evening that he needed sufficient evidence. He wants to make sure the First Nation officials are not walking into a trap. Without his word, no one from the First Nation, who are now waiting in their ships in the nearest lands, will step foot in Jalika. And I am guessing the folks from the Second Nation at this moment are also waiting for the exact confirmation from our unconscious visitor. What we need is proof." With those words, Angla got up from the bed and left the room.

"What do you need to do tomorrow?" the Devil asked the Little Brother without looking at him.

"I planned to visit my friend Katmayo's house and check on his wife. Then maybe try to find out what happened to him."

She nodded, and then said, "Angla said that the two Brothers came with him, so maybe you can ask them to look for your friend while the Elder Brother works with his contacts. Once you are done here, then you can join them."

The Little Brother nodded. "Do you want me to keep an eye on the visitor next room and talk to him once he wakes up?"

"Yes, and in the meantime, talk to that historian again and find what you can about the prince's wife. How is it that no one knows anything about her when she is soon to become the queen? That historian was close to the king and he might know details about the prince's marriage. We should find out what her motive is."

"You seem to be sure about her," he commented, observing the Devil closely.

"There is something about her, something quite out of place, like she is away somewhere else even when she is here. I know that feeling, because I spent half my life living like that."

The Little Brother stilled; she had never spoken of her past before. Whatever small glimpse he got was from her relationship with the king, which she rarely spoke of, and from her interaction with Angla and the minister.

He asked her slowly, "What was Angla talking about? He seemed to think you have some prejudice against the prince's wife."

"He will come around," was all she said, before motioning towards his book and the papers.

He picked them from the table and spread them back on the bed and they started working again. On one page, they understood the scribbling to be instructions on sending a letter to an official in the Second Nation. When the Little Brother put it aside, the Devil said, "If they planned to send a letter on their own after killing the visitor, they would still need a seal, wouldn't they? I'll find out from Angla where the visitor's belongings were dumped and search through them."

It was clear from what they deciphered further that something big was planned, involving casualties from the First Nation at the Peace Events. But try as they might, going through all the drawings and the scribbling again, they couldn't get a hint of what the plan was. It was late in the night when the Devil finally squared up to leave. She did not say anything to the Little Brother; they both knew what was at stake.

35. The Jewel Princess

The Little Brother walked into his room at the Medica, late in the evening, and found the Devil asleep on his bed. When he shut the door and turned back, the Devil opened her eyes and quickly sat up. She looked at him and then relaxed.

"Sorry if I woke you," the Little Brother said. "Have you been here long?"

"I came just a while ago. I was dead tired, so I took a quick nap. I had to wake up early to track the princess's movements."

"You observed her all day? What did you find out?"

"Nothing, it was just like Angla said. She barely spoke to anyone the whole day. She just went about her routine without a glimpse astray."

"So, what's her routine?" the Little Brother asked, sitting on the bed.

"Well, I found out that she goes for a walk in the gardens in the morning and has her breakfast there. So, I reached the prince's quarters and followed her to the gardens. She walked there alone for about an hour, slow, with her head bowed down. She has her own spot in the garden, complete with a dining table and three chairs. Two maids came to serve her and they left after she ate. She then took out a parchment and started making drawings of jewelry. She was there for almost another two hours, and after that, she headed straight to the smithy.

"I must say, of all the people living in the palace, I think she's the only one leading a royal life. She walked to the smithy alone, without greeting a single person on her way. People she came across just did a small bow and moved away to let her pass, and she didn't even spare them a glance. The only place I've seen her as a common person was her new smithy. I wonder what she did before the smithy was set up."

The Devil got up from the bed and walked to the window. After a few minutes, the Little Brother joined her. Both of them stood side by side, looking out the window. The palace was preparing for the crowning ceremony and the inauguration of the Peace Events. Visitors from both the sides were at their last rest stations, the mainlands closest to the ports of Jalika, ready to set out that night.

"The minister, Nayak, and Angla had a meeting with the envoy. They discussed at length the recent events," the Little Brother said. "The envoy had, in the end, agreed to let his people set forth to Jalika, but he is still skeptical about the peace treaty. He said that they should simply turn away and negotiate with Jalika later, when the situation is more stable. It would be catastrophic for us, because even with a small incite, they could annihilate Jalika. So, the minister requested the envoy to meet the visitor from the Second Nation and find out the truth on his own."

"And the Second Nation?" the Devil asked.

"The visitor was mellow in the morning. He agreed that he had made a mistake by trusting that servant and that he wouldn't be posting the letter he wrote earlier. But he will post another one by tonight or he will miss the deadline his master gave him. So, he is drafting a new one now. After dinner, I'll post it for him. Did you find out where his belongings were dumped? We need to find his seal."

"Angla told me that his trunk was moved to one of the new rooms downstairs in case he needed it," the Devil answered. "I'll go fetch it when you talk to him later. I hope Angla made some progress with the maid or we do not have much else to go on."

"Was the maid with the princess any time during the day?" the Little Brother asked. "She was supposed to be her only assistant, after all."

"No, she wasn't with her in the morning; she wasn't with her in the smithy either. After returning from the gardens, the princess handed over her drawings to the smiths and looked at some of the sketches made by them and some sent over by smiths from outside the palace. She then had a small conversation with them on the making and looked at some freshly made pieces. She retired to her quarters after that and was shortly joined by the prince."

The Little Brother turned away from the window and looked at the Devil, but there was no change in her expression. She too looked at him and continued, "Arrangements were being made in the inner gardens while I was waiting outside the quarters. The couple came out, met with the minister and Vihoro near the court hall, and went to the envoy's building. A lunch was arranged for them there. I had a quick lunch myself and waited for them to finish.

"They all walked down and the prince and the minister left immediately. Vihoro and the envoy went into his office. The princess and the envoy's wife came to the inner palace and went into the quarters. After some time, the princess took her to the smithy and spoke to her for a while. Then the envoy's wife left; the princess' maid went behind her carrying a box with some jewelry. The princess herself then worked in the smithy till evening and retired to her quarters just before sundown." The Devil sighed and said, "Her entire day revolves around that jewelry and if it weren't the uneasy feeling in the pit of my stomach, I wouldn't have, even for a second, thought that she is the one weaving evil plots in her head."

"And you still think she's involved with the events happening?" he asked her.

"Yes, I just wish I could find her doing something else besides working on her jewelry. That would give me some clue."

"Well, you cannot blame a jewelry merchant's daughter to be taken up so much with jewelry," he commented and gave a small smile at her surprise.

"After visiting my friend's wife and ensuring that the Brothers will help look for her husband, I went in to have lunch with the historian," the Little Brother said. "I gently broached the subject of the prince being crowned and how Jalika would soon have a new queen. The late king's wife was never interested in that and she never really lived as a queen. Now, however, the case would be different and I asked if he knew anything about her."

"Did he?" the Devil asked him curiously.

"Yes, did you know that she grew up right here in the palace?"

"I guess that's plausible. Before the schools outside were established, a number of kids lived in the palace. But you said she's a jewelry merchant's daughter."

"Not just any jewelry merchant; she is the daughter of the Evil Merchant."

At this, the Devil eyes went wide. Then she looked away, through the window towards the palace again, and said, "Tell me more."

36. The Key

The Little Brother gathered two stools near the window and motioned to the Devil to sit down. He sat opposite to her and told her everything the historian had told him at lunch. The historian had remembered it all well because he had been involved in most of the matters with the king at that time. Only when the minister had decided to settle down from his frequent travels and assumed his position, the historian had retired.

The Evil Merchant was one of the first people to arrive with his family and settle down in Bora. They came from somewhere in the Second Nation after he decided that there was no place for him there. He started out young as a smith and quickly learnt to sell his works for a big profit. He soon became so popular that he started receiving requests from the royals, some even from foreign lands. But he spent so much on acquiring the metal that it bothered him that he wasn't making his sons prosperous. When someone suggested to him to start importing from the islands, he calculated that it would be more profitable to move to Bora. The islands were still new to the trade, unexplored, and without a formal leadership. He hired a few people, and with the help of his sons, setup a huge business. He had seven sons at the time he settled down in Bora, and soon after that, his first daughter was born. He had always wanted a daughter, a muse for the most wonderful of his pieces. His wife had never shown much interest in jewelry, and she was rather like a housemaid who bore children for him. Already weak from the change of place, her condition worsened after her daughter's birth, and she passed away within a few weeks. He doted on his daughter; he built a small workshop for her at home, and for the first time in years since he gave up his business to his sons, he took out his tools. While his business boomed on its own, through his reputation and connections, he quietly taught her everything he knew. But as time passed, he grew restless. In his heart, he always knew that he wanted to be a powerful man, not just famous for his art.

He considered his sons to be his strength; it was through them that he gained and wielded power. They ran the business, hijacked lands, plundered the resources for their own, attacked the Wisalis on his instructions, encouraged many Borans to be goons for them, and lastly took care of the trade for him, ignoring the many warnings they received. They were his strength, but in them, there was no real strength. They were mere puppets to his wicked brain. When the battle started and the attacks came, they threw down their weapons and fled, leaving their father vulnerable to be captured and killed. By the time the war ended, all his sons were taken prisoners. His daughter and a few other relatives were imprisoned in their own mansion as negotiations took place between the Borans and the Wisalis.

The Evil Merchant and his sons had butchered many men, stolen many livelihoods, and gained many enemies. The elders worried that if they weren't killed, they would cause trouble again. And imprisonment was never heard of then in either of the regions. So, the leader of Wisali, who later became the first king, told them to leave Bora and never return. To ensure that they do not cause further trouble, the elders ordered that their family should leave one member behind. The brothers were never close to their sister and were quite jealous of her relationship with their father. Since, they all had their own connections and a future waiting elsewhere, they considered their young sister a burden and decided to leave her in the hands of the king. Since conditions were still unstable in Bora, and the mansion was to be used as a temporary office for running the collective trade, the king decided to bring her to Wisali, where she grew up with the many kids the king and his wife had rescued over the years. After that, no one remembered her to be the Evil Merchant's daughter. When all the children she grew up with picked an avocation and left in pursuit of them, she remained content with being in the palace and not doing anything. So, when it was time for the marriage of the prince, the king had suggested her to be his bride, an already familiar presence in the palace.

The Little Brother finished his story and the Devil immediately asked, "How old was she when her father died?"

"The historian couldn't remember her age, but recollecting her face and height, he said she must've been ten to twelve years old."

"And she never displayed anger or hatred towards the people who killed her father?"

"No, except for one outburst when she was told that she needed to leave her father's workshop. When the king's helper asked her whether they should bring her tools along, she screamed and destroyed all the jewelry she possessed. She then vowed that she would never touch her tools or work on jewelry, ever again. After that, she became reticent and never spoke a word unless absolutely necessary."

"She certainly has broken her vow now," the Devil said. "And if anyone in this palace has a strong motive to bring down the king and his ideals, it's her."

"Yes, I agree," the Little Brother said. "But again, we have the same problem as before; we do not have any proof."

"Have you told Angla this?" the Devil asked.

"Yes, he came late in the morning to see if you were here, and he dined with me and the historian. He was already feeling bad about not listening to you last night, and after listening to the story, he seemed convinced about your suspicion. He's busy with the arrangements for tomorrow and the day after, but he said he would immediately speak to the maid when she is still in the palace. He wants to spook her enough so she would run scared. Since he would be busy and could not possibly help us, he would tell her that he had a suspicion that he was checking on his own and looking for proof to go to his higher command. That way, even if she warns the people she's working with, they would keep an eye only on him. The Elder Brother will follow her as soon as she steps out of the palace and see whom she gets in touch with."

"Alright then, we'll wait and see what happens with that," the Devil said and stood up. "Go talk to the visitor and finish the letter. I'll go down and fetch the seal. Then we'll see if we can sneak into the prince's quarters. Since the prince used to be away most of the time, his wife had the place to herself all this while. It is possible that we might find something there."

After that, the Devil left the room and made her way downstairs, toward the room where the visitor's trunk was dumped. She took out the key that Angla had given her the day before and smiled when she realized that she was opening a lock with a key after a long time.

37. Dangerous and Missing

The Devil walked into the small windowless room where the visitor's trunk was deposited and left the door open to let some light in. She found the trunk in the corner next to the door and bent down to open it. She pushed aside the clothes and other items blindly, but after that, she proceeded with caution, mindful of the arrows that had almost hurt the Little Brother. After a few moments of rummaging in the dark, her eyes strained on the trunk's contents, and she touched the small wooden box that she came for. When she opened the box, to her surprise, it was empty. It matched the description that the Little Brother had given, but there was no sign of the letters or the seal. She searched through the trunk but did not find any other box. After a moment of inspiration, she held the box up and shook it. To her delight, it rattled. She observed it carefully and discovered a small hidden cabinet in the back. She slid the cabinet out and found the seal inside. She took it out, put the cabinet back in, and left the box in the trunk. Then she stepped out of the room, locked it, and took the stairs. She reached the corridor where the Little Brother was staying, but this time she knocked on the door next to his. The Little Brother opened it, and on seeing her, moved away to let her in.

The visitor was sitting on the edge of his bed, bent towards the table on the side, writing the letter. He saw the Devil enter and hand over the seal to the Little Brother and turned back to his letter. Then he commented dryly without looking up, "You found the seal; looks like I hadn't hidden it well after all."

The Devil stepped closer to him and said, "If I may ask, why did you hide it like that?"

"I saw the servant eying my trunk when he came to fill water in my wash room. So, I decided to hide the seal and the letters as they would give away the purpose of my visit. I slid the seal into the cabinet and the letters into the box, locked it carefully, and placed it deep inside my trunk."

"But the box was not locked, and the letters weren't there," she informed him.

He looked up and stared at her with a dead face. His face fell and then he looked down to his letter again, "Well, I guess my efforts were futile then. When I trained in fighting, I should've also gathered some lessons in concealment."

"The trunk must've been thrown aside during the ride. It is possible that the box opened and the letters fell out," the Devil told him gently, and then offered, "I can go check again while you finish the letter."

She turned back to leave. She was almost out of the door when something the visitor said triggered her memory of the Little Brother describing his experience with the visitor's trunk. She rushed back into the room.

"Your arrows," she asked out loud, her eyes trained on the visitor, "they are a mark of the royal court of the Second Nation. Where are they now?"

He looked at her sharply and said, "In my trunk, where I kept them. My master strictly told me to be diligent in using them, so I have not taken them out yet. I had all but forgotten about them until now. I bound them together in leather and placed them at the bottom of my trunk along with the bow. Why do you want to know?"

"No reason. Please continue with your letter, I'll leave now." She gestured at the Little Brother to step outside and walked out.

"What's wrong, did you not see the arrows in the trunk?" the Little Brother asked her.

"I did not. But it was dark and I wasn't looking for them. I'll go check for them now, but I have a feeling that they will be missing, along with the letters."

"Angla said most of the visitor's stuff was put in the visitors building out in the street; maybe they were left there. Why do you think anyone would steal the arrows?"

"They are a mark of the Second Nation. It means the royal court is responsible for any harm that occurs through them. Imagine if they are used to attack a First Nation's official. A war between the two most powerful kingdoms in Khaga will start right here in Jalika."

The Little Brother turned pale and the Devil told him firmly, "Go inside. Finish that letter and get it posted. Then come to Angla's quarters. I will search the trunk again, check the visitor's room outside, and then meet you there."

The Devil then traced her steps back to the room downstairs, but before that, she took the lantern from the Little Brother's room along with her. She opened the lock and bent down to the trunk again. She placed the lantern next to the trunk on the floor and started removing each item from the trunk one by one, till she hit the bottom. The arrows were definitely missing; his bow, however, was still there. There was nothing else in the room for her to look at. So, she locked it back and walked out of the Medica. She headed to the visitor's room, which the Brothers were using as a rest place.

There was no one in the house when she went there and the guard hesitated to let her in. So, she produced the key that Angla had given her the day before and he allowed her to go in. She entered a wide hall, with two rooms each on either side. The ones on the right looked like they were being used by the Brothers and the ones on the left were locked. In a corner of the hall, a small trunk, a few bags, and other items were all piled together neatly. She approached them and went through them all, one after the other. As she had guessed, there was no sign of the letters, and nothing there was big enough to hold the arrows. She peeped into both the open rooms to see if she missed anything, and then left the hall. She locked the door, nodded to the guard, and walked towards the palace. She headed straight to Angla's quarters and found the Little Brother there.

As soon as she entered, the Little Brother said, "I met Angla near the main entrance and informed him about the missing arrows. He had spoken to the maid, but he didn't tell me what happened as he suddenly remembered that he had to do something. He said he would meet us here in a short while." After the Devil nodded, he asked her, "The arrows are definitely missing?"

"Yes, and so are his letters," she answered in a plain tone. The Little Brother did not say anything and both of them waited silently. A little later, Angla walked in with a serious expression, and they immediately knew there was more trouble.

38. A Fool's Heart

"What happened now?" the Little Brother asked Angla.

"Nothing we can do anything about now," Angla replied, and sat down alongside them on the bed. "As per schedule, another batch of that poisonous mineral should have been brought to the palace today. The prince, who would have come today, to be in time for the Peace Events, if it weren't for the king's death, should have brought it with him."

"So, he didn't get it because he came earlier than expected?" the Devil asked.

"No, the prince brought it and handed it over." Looking at the surprised expressions on their faces, Angla went on to explain, "The day I found out that the first batch was stolen, I asked Rola if the prince had checked in the second batch, as I was unsure because he came to the palace unscheduled. Rola told me that the prince didn't, and I left it at that. But today, when the Little Brother told me about the missing arrows, it suddenly occurred to me that I should've checked with the prince too. So, I went to ask him and sure enough, he told me that he had handed it over to a man Rola had sent to collect it. The prince too forgot about it after that. The day of his father's death was still a blur to him for the most part and he did not clearly notice who the man was. He must've thought it truly was from Rola because no one else other than Rola and I knew the schedule."

"Then how did they find out that the prince had brought the second batch of that poison with him that day?" the Little Brother asked.

"I thought about it too. All the packages taken from our mines are logged, but they are kept a secret and sometimes given misguiding names so that common folk would not come to know of them. But we also have a policy in the palace that people entering the inner palace, especially from long distances, should write down the list of any harmful items that they carry with them. The prince, in his hurry, came directly to the inner palace and wrote down exactly what he was carrying. If these people already knew about the mineral, then it wouldn't be too hard to guess that that's what the prince had brought in with him. Both the batches were stolen on the same day and Rola should have damn well checked."

Neither of them said anything to that. Angla closed his eyes, he was dead tired. The Devil and the Little Brother looked at him and then at each other. They knew what would happen if something was done with the poison that was brought by the prince himself.

"What happened with the maid?" the Devil asked Angla after a short pause.

"Since I am busy with work here, I wouldn't be able to assist you both much. So I decided to draw the attention to myself. I met her by the kitchens and casually asked her questions about the prince's wife."

Angla got up from his bed, removed his shirt, splashed cold water on his face, and sat down again with water dripping down his chin. He then continued, "I told her that I found out about the history of the prince's wife, and based on my own investigation of the recent events, the prince's wife could be at the center of an attack on the family members of the king. I also told her that I guessed that the princess's brothers were involved with the bandits. Only, I didn't have enough proof to go to my higher authorities because they would skin me alive if I went accusing the soon-to-be queen of Jalika."

"And what did she say to that?" the Little Brother asked.

"At first she was reticent, but I told her that I would find the end to this sooner or later and it would better for her if she cooperated. I also warned her that I would simply throw her out of the palace right at that moment if she didn't talk, which I had the complete power to do. I could tell she wanted to bash my head in, but she knew I was the second in command of security, so she started to speak, with enough restraint to convince me. She told me that the prince's wife had always hated her husband's family who snatched her away from her own and brought her here to be raised amongst peasants. She hated that the king got her married to his stupid miner of a son. So, the princess simply wanted to escape from here and reach her brothers. She added that she did not know anything about the bandits."

"That's all? She didn't say anything else?" the Devil asked.

"Yes, that was all. I couldn't question her further as I had my summons to be somewhere else, and people were already eyeing us with suspicion in the kitchens. So, I had to let her go. But she did give us some important news."

"About the princess's brothers you mean?" the Little Brother wondered.

"And her escape," the Devil added. "If she wanted to cause trouble here, she must've planned an escape for herself to be out of here in time. That could be why she collaborated with the bandits."

"If the maid was hiding more, then why did she give away that part? Couldn't she have come up with a lie?" the Little Brother questioned.

This time Angla answered him, "It is possible that the maid has the bandits' best interests at heart and not the princess's. Maybe the bandits are using the princess just to get information and implement their plans. Then they wouldn't care if she escaped or not, hell they may not even have an escape ready for her. The whole thing could have been just to fool her into helping them."

"She didn't seem a fool to me," the Devil commented.

"Well, the bandits must've convinced her somehow, maybe by showing her a few fake trinkets from her brothers; they seem resourceful enough," Angla told her.

The Devil remained silent after that and thought hard, as did the other two.

Then Angla said, "I've put a shadow to her inside the palace. Once she leaves here, the Elder Brother will follow her. She's bound to reach out to whoever is planning with her. But it may be dangerous for the Elder Brother to do this alone. So, I found out where her house is, maybe I should go stake it out first."

"You are tired and you need to be out there in a few hours for the crowning ceremony. You can't leave now," the Devil told him.

"Yes. I'll go," the Little Brother stood up and announced. "I've been holed up here for too long. Let me find the Elder Brother. I will come back as soon as we find some information."

"All right, you do that," the Devil said. "Angla will provide you the directions to her house. I wanted to sneak into the prince's quarters, but it's too risky now; only a few hours for the crowning to start. I'll do it during the ceremony when everyone's away."

Angla looked at her once before turning away. He told the Little Brother what he needed to know and watched him depart in a hurry. He turned back and stood looking at the Devil stretched out on his bed.

39. The Vigil Continues

Outside the palace, Little Brother walked along the southern wall till half its length and turned right. He headed towards the village where the princess's maid lived. It was a small village, with newly built buildings in the beginning occupied mostly by palace workers and old ones at the end occupied by farmers. The Little Brother walked towards the south-east end, as per the directions given by Angla.

The maid's farm was on the end of a narrow road, which ran from the center of the village to the border of the huge plantations and farms maintained by the palace. There were houses on either side of the road, but there were no lights, and the Little Brother could hear his own footsteps echoing in the silence. At the end of the road, he crossed the street and noticed movement ahead of him. The Elder Brother came into view, caught the Little Brother by his elbow, and dragged him lightly to a spot on the right from where there was a clear view of the maid's little hut. Like the other houses, there was no light inside, and they couldn't hear any movements either.

"She started out late from the palace and headed straight here. She has come out a few times, to get water from the well, to feed the chicken, to clean up, and then to collect logs. She locked her door and dimmed the lantern about three hours ago. There hasn't been any movement since." The Elder Brother quickly summarized for the Little Brother's benefit and asked, "What news do you have?"

The Little Brother told him about the Devil's findings, the princess's history, the missing arrows, and Angla's missing poison.

The Elder Brother looked grave and said, "This is worse than I thought. We at least know now that the princess may be involved, but we are nowhere near establishing the proof."

"What are the other Brothers up to?" the Little Brother asked him.

"The Second Brother told me that the allies have started arriving. The Second Nation folks have also set out from the mainland and would reach the Second Palace by tomorrow afternoon. They will set out to the Main Palace in the evening. The other Brothers have been tracking some rogue hunters from the tribes, regarding whom there have been many rumors, but so far they haven't found them. That reminds me, I need to leave them a message. Also, I have to check in with a friend of mine who lives in the next street."

"Alright, I will wait here," the Little Brother told him. "You go ahead."

The Elder Brother nodded at him and left. The Little Brother looked back at the hut. It was as still and dark as before. He figured that she must be asleep and moved closer. He went around the hut to see if there was any other path to leave the place. Except for a small drain through which water from the house was released into the farm, there was no sign of a trail. He walked to the single cleaning room on the side, a little to the left of the hut. It was small, with just a bucket, a huge container of water, and a pile of old clothes. On the other side of the room, towards the front, there was a track leading to the nearby well.

He returned to his old spot and sat down staring at the hut again. A little more than an hour passed when he suddenly opened his eyes and realized that he had fallen asleep. He shook his head and sat up straight. A short while later, he heard movement inside the hut and saw the old door open. The maid walked out and went about her activities normally. When she left with her container to get water, he considered entering the hut to inspect it, but she returned soon and did not leave again. She finished her bath and was preparing food on the cooking stones outside the hut when the Elder Brother tapped on the Little Brother's shoulder. She looked up at the sound of the Little Brother's gasp, and the Elder Brother motioned the Little Brother to stay silent and hidden. He then bent down, pulling the Little Brother with him, and whispered in his ear.

"She will soon leave for the palace. You follow her from a safe distance. I will stay back here to inspect the place. Then I will have to meet the other Brothers at the visitor's room outside the Medica. We will all come to meet you after that."

The Little Brother nodded at him and they both waited for her to finish and leave. It was still a little dark and the sun was hiding shyly on the horizon. The Little Brother, who earlier felt tired crouching alone, smiled when he felt the early morning breeze on his face. He saw the maid lock the hut, leave some grain for her chicken, and walk toward the road. As soon as she crossed the street, the Elder Brother nodded at the Little Brother to leave.

The Little Brother followed the maid from a safe distance such that he could keep an eye on her and yet stay hidden in case she turned back. She walked out of the village, silent and alone, in quick small steps, until she reached the palace wall. There, she took the turn before the southern wall of the palace. But at the intersection of the lanes, two coming out of the other two villages and one leading to the market, she met a man briefly in the corner. Just as the Little Brother got a glance of him, the man smiled at the maid and walked away toward the market. It all happened in a few seconds and the maid continued walking towards the palace at her steady pace. The Little Brother, sure that he had seen that man before, ran in the direction of the market to see if he could catch a glimpse of him. But the man had already disappeared. So the Little Brother got back to his original path quickly and reached the Main Gate, where he saw the maid enter through the half-open gate rather than the workers' door. She went straight to the kitchens, arranged a breakfast tray, and took it to the prince's quarters. The Little Brother saw her disappear inside and turned back. He immediately saw the young man whom Angla had assigned to follow the maid inside the palace. Nodding at him, he left the inner palace and walked towards Angla's room.

As he opened the door, he saw the Devil waiting to leave and Angla was nowhere to be seen.

"Heading out now?" he asked her.

"Yes, I snuck into the smithy earlier, but found nothing other than jewelry designs. Angla had gone to see the prince earlier; he told me the smiths usually come early. As soon as the prince and his wife leave for the court hall, I will talk to the smiths and probe them to see what I can find out. Angla is with the chief and the minister, overseeing things in the hall. He will not be able to keep an eye on little things; you should head there."

The Little Brother nodded at her and watched her leave. He then cleaned up, changed his clothes, and headed out again.

40. A New Beginning

By the time the Devil reached the inner palace, the prince and his wife had already left for the court hall. The whole place was swarmed with workers, running about their errands. The Devil reached the small lawn outside the hall in the prince's quarters and saw a man leave the smithy with some drawings in his hand. Two men were working inside the smithy and she quickly remembered that only two smiths were hired to work there.

She approached the door and knocked on it before entering the smithy. Both the smiths looked up at her. One turned back to his work and continued silently while the other asked her what she wanted. She told him that Angla had asked her to keep a check on the comings and goings in the inner palace and she did not know the person who just left the smithy with a sheaf of papers.

"He's one of the smiths who work in his own place outside the palace," the smith informed her.

"I thought it was just the two of you who work here with the princess," the Devil commented. "I didn't know that smiths from outside come in as well. How many more are there?"

"There is only one other than the man you saw, but this one is fairly regular. He comes in every day," the smith told her. "I wonder why he wasn't hired," he added, more to himself, than to her.

"What do you mean?" the Devil asked, her curiosity piqued.

"Well, there were seven of us who were chosen to meet the princess when she wanted to hire smiths. Veera, the guy whom you saw earlier, was by far the most experienced and the most talented of us all. He had worked with famous people in the Second Nation before he came to settle here in Wisali."

"Can you guess why he wasn't hired?" the Devil asked, quelling her urge to run after that man, who must've already left the inner palace by then.

"He already has a large smithy of his own and I think the princess thought it would be best if he continued to work there," the smith said. "So, she told him to come in here once in a while, to leave a few designs of his that she might find interesting."

"Oh, but I saw him leave with something," the Devil probed.

"He never gets to meet the princess and he only guesses at what she might like. He wasn't sure of some of his new designs and so took them back with him. He said that he would drop them off after the crowning ceremony if he changes his mind."

"If he comes back here again after the crowning ceremony, could you ask him to wait for me?" the Devil asked the smith. "I want to talk to him."

The smith nodded at her and she thanked him. She then left the smithy and arrived at the court hall. The prince, his wife, his sisters, the council members, and their seconds had just finished a short meeting in the council room and were ready to move to the court hall, where many people had gathered to see the crowning ceremony. When she headed there, she noticed that a large crowd was already present. Even the corridors were full, with people trying to look in through the windows. Still, many people were waiting outside in the grounds to hear the prince as their king for the first time.

Owing to her small height, the Devil couldn't see well above the heads of the crowd. So, she looked up for vantage points, but the balcony and the corridor on the first floor were all completely occupied too. The only people sitting were the ones in the balcony, and she noticed the envoy Merin, his wife, the visitor from the Second Nation Riccham, a few officials working in different islands, and a few others whom she couldn't recognize. She wondered if she could observe from behind them, but then realized that that would be too far from the dais. Then she looked at the many small officials and other palace workers standing in the corridors on either side of the balcony and wondered if she could squeeze in there. Just then, she felt a hand on her shoulder and turned to see the Little Brother. He motioned her to follow him and stepped out of the hall. The Devil followed him outside. He led her around the hall, into the inner palace, and she asked him where they were going.

"Have you noticed that the corridors on the first floor end halfway on either side of the hall? Angla told me about these rooms that were newly made out of the closed corridors on the first floor around the dais. You know there is a tradition in many courts where the royal family members watch from behind shuttered windows for safety. In some places, it's the only way the women folk are allowed to observe a ceremony. So, to accommodate such tradition for any visitors, the minister had special rooms built in our court hall too. I was looking from there when I noticed you down here. Come quickly, they must be starting anytime soon."

The Little Brother was excited. It was the first time any kind of a ceremony had ever happened in Jalika. He had never witnessed any ceremonies since his childhood, even during his travels. By being there then, it felt like he was a part of a little piece of Jalika's history. He found the small staircase from the inner palace that snaked its way upstairs towards the court hall. On the first floor, they reached a narrow perpendicular corridor that had two heavy set doors on either side of its wall. The Little Brother reached the one closest to them and pushed it. They entered a dark empty hall that extended ahead and to the right of the door and then further left at the end. The hall surrounded the dais below on three sides.

The Devil noticed two huge rectangle shaped openings on the wall facing the dais from the left, three on the wall directly behind the dais and two on the other side. The openings were covered with transparent curtains, which the Devil thought were a part of the decoration when she had noticed them from below. They took one opening each and looked down. The dais, which had been empty before, was completely occupied now. In the center, the prince sat on a very fashionable throne, and the Devil almost sniggered out loud when she saw his uncomfortable posture. On either side of him, two similar chairs were occupied, left by the minister and right by his wife. On either side of the dais, were three rows of similar looking couches. The ones on the left to the prince, after the minister, were occupied by the council members. The prince's sisters, his brother-in-law, his father's sister, her husband, and their son were sitting on the first two rows of the couches to his right. Angla was sitting in the last row alone. Suddenly, he looked up from below, straight at the Devil, winked, and looked back towards the dais again when the minister stood up. The hall went silent and the crowning ceremony began.

41. The Other Smith

The minister started the ceremony with a small note about the dead king and proceeded to talk about the role the king's family played in building Jalika. He then went on to mention how many of Jalika's current mining resources were discovered by the prince himself. While he talked, the Devil carefully observed the dais. The prince and most others were looking at the minister. Some were looking at the crowd, some sat with their heads bent down to their lap, and some, like the princess, were staring blandly in no particular direction. Just like all the seating on the dais, the princess's chair was slightly turned towards the center of dais, towards the prince, but was still facing the crowd.

The princess stared somewhere above the prince's chair, but only her head was turned that way. The rest of her body was inclined towards the crowd, and she sat ramrod straight. Even when the prince got up from his chair to stand next to the minister, she didn't change her position. Only her neck moved, following the prince's movements, and her eyes rested on his back. This intrigued the Devil; she observed her for a few more minutes to confirm that the princess maintained her body tight, unmoving, and aimed at the crowd all the time. The princess was wearing a blood red silk sari and three lines of heavy set gold jewelry around her neck. She was the only one the Devil ever saw wearing a silk sari every day; rather unusual for someone living in the tropical climate of Jalika. Women on the islands wore saris only on special occasions and silk ones were almost never seen. But, it was the jewelry that caught the Devil's eye.

The Devil moved towards the Little Brother's window to get a better look at the princess's jewelry. Too engrossed in listening to the ceremony, he simply walked to the window she had abandoned, and continued to listen. As she observed the princess's jewelry, the Devil considered the princess; a jewelry merchant's beloved daughter, the one who vowed to never touch her tools again, recently opened a smithy and hired men to work for her. There must be a reason for the princess's sudden interest in a skill that she had given up as a child. The Devil craned her neck to get a better look at the jewelry, but even from her new position, she couldn't decipher their patterns. From where she was standing, there was no way she could get a better look. Guessing that the jewelry must be on display for someone in the crowd, the Devil focused in that direction. She scanned the lines of people standing opposite to her for anyone particularly looking at the princess. When she couldn't find any one, she left that side of the hall, walked the length of it from behind the dais, and reached the other side. She walked to the nearest open spot and looked at the crowd on the other side. She almost missed him once because of his bent head, but when he lifted it again to look at the princess before bending down once more, she caught him. He was constantly swiveling his head between the princess and a parchment in his hand. Careful to not get unwanted attention, the Devil waved at the Little Brother from the other side, to catch his eye. When he finally noticed her, she motioned him to come to her side. She then looked back at the dais to verify that she wasn't noticed by anyone. The ceremony was coming to an end with the prince making a statement about his duties. She looked back at the crowd, trying to find the same bent head, but the man had disappeared.

Cursing, she turned to the Little Brother who arrived at her side and said, "Listen, I think the princess is working with someone other than the bandits. Apart from the two smiths who work with her in the palace, she hired two more men from the outside, who come here to leave their designs. One of them comes in everyday. His name is Veera, and he settled in Wisali recently after a successful profession somewhere in the Second Nation. The princess seems to be communicating with him through her jewelry, and he seems to respond to her using his designs that he drops off. I shall leave now to go and find him. You must let the Elder Brother know about this and ask him to find out about this smith. Then, you find Angla and let him know about this as well."

Satisfied with his nod, despite his stunned expression, she rushed out of the hall, wound her way through the narrow inner corridor, then the staircase, and ran towards the smithy. She found the same two smiths again, engrossed in their work, and there was no sign of the other smith. She entered without knocking and asked the smith who had spoken to her earlier.

"Didn't Veera just come to drop off his designs? I have a note for him from the princess. She's busy with the ceremony, and when she found out that I had seen him here earlier, she sent me back with a message."

"Sorry, dear. He just left. If you rush, you might catch him before he leaves the palace."

"There is too much crowd, I cannot hope to find him before he leaves," the Devil told him. "Can you let me know where he lives please?"

A few minutes later, the Devil was walking out of the palace on her way to Veera's house. When she saw that she couldn't make her way past the crowd and through the main gate, she took a detour. She walked out past the gardens and came around to the nearest village, after the plantations on the north end of the palace. She came to the road that went from the main gate of the palace, through the main buildings nearby, and through the villages. She reached the first village on that road and was amazed at the sight of the many abandoned huts and small buildings around. The village once started at the end of the plantations of the palace and covered the entire distance where the many new palace buildings stood. But, after the area was designated to the palace, many people moved to better places, some even built their houses in the middle of their own farms. Only the old houses, deep into the center of the village, away from the road, remained as they once were.

She crossed the center and emerged on the other side. The place had a few houses scattered with large distances between them. Most of them were newly built in the area between the village and the school and manufacturing units and merged with the Chama forest. She got lost in the maze of narrow turns but finally found her way out of the edge of the fields toward a long, rough, trail that led to the large house she was looking for.

The house stood alone on elevated land with thick tall trees covering it on three sides. There was an open shed on one side of the trail in front of the house, and the other side had a small stable where a carriage and two horses were present. A bullock cart stood in front of the house and it was being loaded with bags and trunks by four servants alternatively.

She found a tall tree on the trail within seeing distance from the house and climbed it up quickly. She crouched on a branch, leaned towards the house, and took out her spyglass. She pointed it at the house and looked into each room that was visible from her position.

42. Light and Dark

Crouched on the tree branch, the Devil could see that the four servants were carrying their load down from the first floor through the stairs in the left-most room. As she watched, they made two such rounds, and then two of them came out to arrange the carriage, while the other two carried stuffed bags from the verandah toward it. They fed the horses and the oxen tied to the bullock cart and then went around the house to the back.

As the shed, the animals, and their carriages blocked her view of the ground floor, the Devil focused on the floor above. The first floor had four rooms, and based on the furniture, the Devil concluded that the one on the extreme left was a work room. Beside that room was a hall and then a bedroom. The room on the extreme right did not have a window or any other opening for the Devil to look into. She turned her focus back to the work room where she could see Veera standing. When she moved to the hall, through the two long windows, she noticed someone going out of the hall through the door on the other side. The person returned after a while and went into the bedroom. The curtains were partly drawn in the bedroom and she couldn't see what he was up to.

After a short while, she saw the same person, a tall and well-built shape, walk back into the hall from the bedroom and leave the same way as before. He emerged outside from behind the house and walked towards the horse carriage. The Devil was clear that he was not one of the servants that she had seen earlier. He checked the carriage and closed its door from behind. He then walked to the bullock cart and checked the items that were loaded. He got onto the cart at the front and guided the oxen out of the yard and toward the trail. The Devil shifted to lie down on the branch and slid a little to the other side to keep out of sight, but the man didn't look up from his straight course and soon disappeared from the trail. She slid back into her position and focused her glass on the ground floor, now that a gap had been created with the cart gone. She saw that Veera was now downstairs on the last step of the inner staircase, which seemed to lead straight from his work room above into a workshop of sorts below. Most of the ground floor seemed to be used as a smithy, with oily walls, greasy floor, and tools lying around haphazardly.

When he disappeared deep into the house where she couldn't see him, the Devil decided that it was time for her to explore further and climbed down the tree. Staying on one side of the trail and ducking behind the trees, she walked towards the house and reached the yard. She went around the yard till the end of the verandah on the right. She then moved to the window on the side wall of the house and looked in. Just on the right of the window was a small cooking place, and on the left, a small room. The rest of the ground floor was, just like she had guessed, a smithy. She saw Veera come down the stairs on the far end, and there was no sign of the servants. She ducked from the window and ran to the back of the house. There she found the outdoor stairs that led to the hall on the upper floor.

She ran up the stairs lightly, approached the open door of the hall through the length of the small balcony, and waited for a moment at the entrance. She could faintly hear footsteps and small thumps from below, but there were no other noises. So, she stepped in and looked around. Whether the furniture and other belongings were already removed, or it was never decorated at all, the room was bare. The door to her right that led to the work room was closed, and she didn't approach it as Veera could walk in anytime from the inner stairs. She looked at the open door towards the bedroom on her left and walked in. Like the hall, the bedroom was almost bare. An empty closet stood open on one side and a small table beside it, with a few portraits and a small locked box on top of it.

The Devil walked to the table and picked up the portraits. The first one had an old painting of an elderly couple. The woman's face strongly resembled that of Veera except for his nose, which resembled that of the man. The second portrait was of a strongly built man, sitting on a throne-like chair, with a younger looking Veera and a woman, perhaps his wife, standing behind him. The woman had the same grey eyes as the man sitting in the chair. The Devil picked up the last portrait; it was of Veera and his wife, holding a small boy of maybe two or three years. As she placed the portraits back, the Devil wondered what happened to Veera's family.

The locked box looked complicated to open, so the Devil first walked to the open closet and looked for clues as to what it might've contained. But it seemed to have been wiped, and there were no traces left. However, when she pulled out a drawer in the middle of the closet, she found something—a small, wooden framed portrait. In the portrait, a young boy of maybe six or seven, a young girl who looked a few years older than the boy, and a man of maybe fifty years old, were all working in a smithy. Even on the fuzzy, old paper, the Devil could recognize that the man was the dead Evil Merchant. It was a portrait of him with his daughter and an apprentice working together. The missing pieces of the story fell in place in the Devil's mind about the relationship between the princess and Veera and how they must be communicating using jewelry. They must have known each other's style since childhood, and it was an excellent way to stay connected without falling prey to the watching eyes of the palace members as well as the bandits, who must be keeping her under strict scrutiny.

When she was about to look further, the Devil heard footsteps a little louder and figured that Veera must be in his work room. Her eyes went to the closed door leading to the next room, which she couldn't look into before. As she pushed it open, a faint stench of oil reached her and it grew thick as she stepped inside. The room was dark and it took a while for her eyes to adjust. She found a small bench covered in blankets and pillows next to the wall, and she assumed that the room must have been in use by the heavy man who had left with the bullock cart earlier.

As she took a few steps further inside, her foot touched something soft, and she looked down. There she found the four servants lying unconscious, and even in the dark, the Devil could see that there was blood on them in some places. She hadn't noticed them when she entered the room because she had covered her mouth and nose to the smell and was trying to focus her eyes. When she bent down to feel the pulse on the nearest servant, she slipped and realized that the floor was covered in oil. She tried to stand up but slipped again. Cursing, she removed her hand from her face and pushed herself up with both hands. But before she could stand up, a thick wooden log hit her hard on the head, and she turned to see a dangerously serious Veera standing over her as she lost consciousness.

43. No Time for Trouble

It took the Little Brother a while to come out of the palace as he made the mistake of approaching the main gate and ended up struggling through the heavy crowd. He sighed in relief as he stepped away from the busy street and turned towards the visitor building. When he arrived there, the guard informed him that the Elder Brother was already in. He went inside and found the Elder Brother writing a note to the Second Brother. He collapsed from exhaustion into a chair next to the Elder Brother and straddled his injured hand as it throbbed from pushing through the crowd.

He was still dazed from the crowning ceremony and was amazed by the wise yet formidable words of both the minister and the new king. In that excitement, the Devil's words hadn't quite registered in his head. But as he narrated them to the Elder Brother, they sunk in and rendered him a delayed shock. The ingenuity of it all, using jewelry to send across messages, so anyone watching her in the palace wouldn't know what she was up to. He was still baffled at the idea that the beautiful, demure princess, now the queen, had managed to fool the king, the minister, the council, and her own husband all these years and was planning a revenge with the bandits while carefully laying out her own escape.

The Elder Brother sat in silence for a few minutes after the Little Brother finished. He then looked at his half-finished note and looked up at the Little Brother who returned the gaze with an expression of doubt. He blinked and told the Little Brother, "Alright, I will find some people in jewelry business at the market and see what they know about this new smith."

"Have you met the other Brothers?" the Little Brother asked him.

"No, they will be leaving a message for me here soon. Have you told Angla about this?"

"Not yet, he was in the ceremony, and there was no way I could get his attention. So, I came here first to let you know."

The Elder Brother nodded and went back to writing his note. The Little Brother got up, gulped down two glasses of water, and made his way back to the palace. The area was still crowded and he couldn't find a way to the gate from his position. He decided to get around the crowd and see if he could find a way from the other side. As he walked away from the gate, he caught a glimpse of the man the maid had spoken to in the morning. The Little Brother had forgotten about him till that moment. He looked again and saw the man walk towards the market once more. Figuring it would take him ages to get to the palace, he ran after the man, determined to catch him.

The market was empty for the most part and the man quickly turned to the darker, narrower lanes at the back. The Little Brother struggled to keep up as he had to stay far enough to not get noticed in the deserted alleyways. At one point, he thought he lost the man, but a left turn and a few steps later, he saw him entering an old building through a small wooden door. The Little Brother parked himself at the edge of a verandah of an old, empty building at the turning and waited. Unconsciously, he picked up two stones lying beside him and started rolling them in his hands.

A while later, the same man came out, but now he was followed by three other men. None of them were wearing black, but the Little Brother noticed the chain with the tiny poison pack around their necks. He stood up and followed them, still rolling the stones in his hands. This time, he did not have to mind his footsteps to be silent as the men were so loud that he could hear their conversation quite clearly.

"What took you so long?" the one at the back asked the man whom the Little Brother had followed.

"You remember that woman who almost caught you in the Chama forest? Well, she was tracking me in the village," the man answered. "I had to get rid of her in the crowd outside the palace before heading out here."

"That's the wife of one of the messengers we killed," the other one at the back answered. "Remember the feisty one?"

"Oh yes, so that's his wife?" said the one next to him, "maybe when we see her next, we should tell her how her husband hopped on a single foot when we cut off his leg."

He was still laughing with his head thrown back when the stone hit him in the shoulder and the laugh turned into a scream. They all turned back to see the other stone from the Little Brother's hand that was already coming at them. It was aimed at the second one at the back, but he turned away in time and it whizzed just past his ear. He then bent down involuntarily expecting another stone, but when he realized there was none, he picked up his friend who had fallen clutching his shoulder. The other men in the front too removed their hands from shielding their face and rushed at the Little Brother.

The Little Brother panicked. He looked around to find a weapon, but there were no sticks or stones nearby. So, he crunched some mud in his fist and threw it at the face of the man coming at him. The man screeched to a halt as the mud hit his eyes, but the other one closed his eyes tightly and hurled himself at the Little Brother who went down crashing on the road. The one who attacked him then moved to sit on him and before the Little Brother could get a grip on the guy's neck, he hit a strong fist at the Little Brother's face. The Little Brother's vision was blinded for a second and he saw stars dance in front of his eyes in broad daylight.

"Is he down?" someone asked in the background.

"Yes, no strength in him," someone else answered. "He seemed to have panicked after throwing those stones. He must not have realized you two were there in front of us."

"Look at the bandages on his head and the hand. Maybe, he is one of those crack heads who pick fights on the streets for no reason."

"Still, we have to be careful till tonight. Let's tie him up and throw him in one of our rooms to be sure."

The Little Brother halted his breathing in order to stop himself from squealing when they tied up his injured hand. Fortunately, his panicked brain started functioning after the blow to his face that almost cracked his skull; a few inches below and it would've broken his jaw. The men thought that he was unconscious. Even if they didn't, he thought he would pretend that the blow broke his jaw and he could talk no more. But as they lifted him up and carried him for a short while before throwing him down, he wished he truly was unconscious. The pain in his face was unbearable, not to mention the vicious throbbing of his hand.

Once he heard the lock click as they left the room, he opened his eyes.

It was dark in the room and he couldn't see anything from his position on the floor. So he closed his eyes again and tried to think of pleasant things to divert his mind from the pain. But the only thoughts were the ones that sent him into panic again. He realized that he hadn't updated Angla, and neither the Devil nor the Brothers knew where he was. As blissful sleep finally crept up on him, he thought about the words of the men after they brought him down; something was going to happen that night.

44. The Way Out

Angla noticed the Devil disappear from his line of sight, and after a short while, saw the Little Brother move away as well. As the minister concluded the ceremony, Angla looked at the stiff profile of the new Queen, and thought about the Devil's words. When he went over the drawings in the Little Brother's book, he could clearly see that there was a plan for an attack at the inauguration of the Peace Events. But the Devil had raised the question of why the tunics were discarded a few days before the event. They wondered if that meant a change from the original plan and what that might turn out to be. Moreover, there was no mention of an escape plan for the queen. Angla didn't realize that the minister had finished until everyone stood up to hail the new king. He too stood up and then fell in line with the council members who were walking behind the king, the queen, and the minister to make a public appearance outside the palace.

As he stepped out of the hall and walked along the way cleared for their free passage, Angla saw Merin, the envoy of the First Nation, his wife Adola and Riccham, the visitor from the Second Nation. As he moved aside at the end of the corridor to let the others go ahead, he thought about the meeting between Merin, the minister, and the prince, where he was also present. He had observed curiously as the minister and the envoy parried with words, while the prince and the envoy's wife supported their respective wards. Merin was smart and pertinent while the minister was wise and patient. It had taken a whole two hours for the minister to convince Merin about what he had earlier informed the prince and Nayak—the involvement of the bandits. While the envoy was convinced of their involvement, he couldn't accept that no one high in the palace had helped them. The minister didn't have an answer to that because he had decided to keep the Devil's suspicions about the princess under wraps even from the prince and Nayak until there was proof. To assuage Merin's fears that there was conspiracy with the Second Nation, Angla had arranged a meeting between Merin and Riccham at the Medica after which both parties agreed that the minister was being framed. Angla was so lost in his thoughts that he didn't realize that Merin came to stand beside him until a few seconds.

"That was quick," the envoy commented. "I expected it to go on for long."

"It's not a celebration really. None of us expected that the prince would have to take his father's position," Angla answered him. "We do not have a formal ritual written down for our ceremonies and of course there is the added hurry because of the Peace Events starting tomorrow."

Angla then saw Riccham arrive beside Merin and addressed him, "Thank you for attending the ceremony despite your injuries. Would you like to return to your room now?"

"Yes, I wish to go back now," the visitor replied. He then asked, "Do you know when the officials from the Second Nation will arrive here?"

"They must have just arrived at the Second Palace and will be resting there for a short while. They shall soon set forth to Wisali and should reach here late in the night."

The visitor nodded and retreated. He told his escort, a young man from Angla's team, to guide him back to his Medica room, and soon disappeared from their sight. After a short pause, Merin's wife, Adola, commented, "So, the Second Nation officials definitely won't be there for tonight's dinner."

Looking at the confused expression on Angla's face, Merin told him, "We were told about it just before the ceremony. The queen has decided to arrange an intimate dinner for the few officials who arrive by evening. She has expressed concern that officials from the Second Nation won't be able to make it on time."

Angla nodded, but before he could question Merin further about the dinner, the king and the other officials returned inside, and everyone was motioned to move for lunch. As the couple moved away, Angla detached from the crowd and walked out. The Devil's words about the change of plans resounded in his head. Added to that, there was the concern of the queen being the chief conspirer. It was possible that an ambush was being planned for the night's dinner. With him questioning the maid and Riccham being rescued and brought to the Main Palace, the perpetrators must've guessed that at least he was onto them and may have preponed their plans.

As he made his way out of the Main Palace, he decided that he should interrogate the maid thoroughly. Since he anyway had to notify the kitchens about sending lunch to the visitor in the Medica room, he headed to the kitchens to see if he could find the young man he had put on the maid's trail inside the palace. He notified the chief cook that the visitor had retired to his room and would need food to be sent to him and his escort. As he turned to leave, Angla found the boy he had assigned to trail the maid. He had a worried expression on his face and was twisting his hands continuously. He looked at Angla and launched into a fast speech.

"I am sorry, sir, but the maid has disappeared. She went to the cleaning rooms and never returned. I waited for almost two hours near the only entrance and even asked another woman to look for her inside, but she seems to have gone somewhere from there without my notice."

"Okay, go back there again and talk to the other maids to see if anyone knows about another escape from there. But before that, call one of your mates and ask him to follow the king and the queen from a safe distance and see if the maid makes an appearance. If she does, notify me immediately."

The boy nodded vigorously and walked away, almost running. Angla sighed and asked one of the minders to provide him a light meal. As he sat down to eat, he had a feeling that it would be the last meal he would have for many more hours to come. If he had to guess, the night was going to be eventful.

45. Help and Hope

The Little Brother floated in and out of consciousness. He wondered how long it had been since he was thrown in that room. After they dumped him, the men stood somewhere close to the room and talked. Though he couldn't see where the window was, he could smell smoke and hear their loud voices that floated in through it. He tried to stay awake to listen to them, but he soon gave in to the blackness that drowned him.

He opened his eyes after a while but immediately closed them again. He could hear murmurs and realized that that was what made him aware. He couldn't remember how long ago it was that the bandits talked outside, but someone was definitely there then, moving just outside his room. Then he heard someone talk and thought he should recognize that voice. It was a familiar voice telling someone that the room was dark and empty and that they should move on. The Little Brother wanted to scream, but when he tried to jerk his mouth open, the cloth tied against his mouth tightened, and all he could manage was a tiny squeak before the blinding pain threatened to make him faint.

A few minutes later, shouts and loud noises rang outside; there was fighting. Though it was risky to get their attention, it seemed like the Little Brother's only option at that moment. Fortunately, his legs were fine and functional even though they were tied. So, he brought them together toward his stomach into a cocoon and heaved himself up into a sitting position. He blinked and focused his eyes. He seemed to be in the middle of a small room with an open window at his back. Half the room was empty while the other half was stocked with what looked like bags of grain. He crawled a little toward the bags and found a small stool, which must have been left there to reach the highest rows of bags. There was an old, battered, and unlit lantern standing on the stool.

He could still hear the shouts and rings from the outside, but the magnitude had gone down a bit. So, he suppressed his pain and crawled toward the stool as quickly as possible. He reached the other side of the stool and when he was within a reaching distance from it, he waited. As soon as the noise died outside and he could hear soft voices, he straightened himself up and with all his strength, kicked the stool violently. It skidded across the room towards the center before falling down and the crash echoed in the room. The push also threw the lantern at the wall near the window, and it smashed into pieces on the floor.

As the noise settled down, he crawled a little bit to be in direct sight of the window, in case someone decided to look in from there instead of opening the door. Sure enough, the Third Brother's face appeared against the light with a shocked expression on his face. As the Third Brother disappeared, the Little Brother tried to move his jaw a bit again and realized that it was not too painful to move. The punch had landed on the right side of his face, in the middle of the cheek, and fortunately hadn't hurt his jaw badly. He heard the Brothers murmur outside and then he saw the Elder Brother's face in the window while the Fourth Brother too looked in from behind. The lock outside the room was broken, and the doors were opened. The Third Brother rushed to him and untied his bindings.

The other Brothers too entered while the Third Brother removed the cloth across the Little Brother's face as he moaned in pain. They lifted him onto the stool that he had kicked earlier and gave him some water to drink. He sipped it slowly while the Brothers patiently waited for him to finish. Then he looked up and asked, still testing his jaw, "How did you arrive at this place?"

"The Brothers were tracking this group of strange men in the Chama forest when Katmayo's wife told us that they were visiting this village often, mostly to take rest, as it looked like," the Elder Brother told him, as the Fourth Brother examined the Little Brother's injured hand and the swollen cheek. "They finally found a bandit making his way here from the Chama forest and followed him. I joined them near the market. When we arrived here, we found three bandits and a villager, whom we guessed as the owner of this property. I presume they are the ones that locked you up?"

The Little Brother nodded and said, "I saw the maid talk to that villager briefly on her way to the palace. After I met you today, I saw the same man again near the gate and followed him to an old closed inn, where he was joined by the other three."

He winced as the Fourth Brother pressed on his cheek and said, "It's a good thing you have plump cheeks."

The Little Brother smiled at his comment and then frowned as he said, "The villager told the bandits that he misguided Katmayo's wife who was on his trail, and they laughed and made fun of how they cut off Katmayo's leg. I got agitated and hurled stones at them, and I ended up here."

"So, these were indeed the ones that killed the messengers," the Third Brother commented and asked, "Why didn't they kill you?"

"They thought I was a madman and did not know that I was following them," the Little Brother answered. He then remembered a bit of their conversation he had heard through the window, "I think they were already worried about killing the messengers. Apparently, their orders were to only modify the messages before they reach the Second Palace."

"Orders from whom?" the Elder Brother asked.

"I do not know. It could be the queen, or her maid, or someone else."

"Did they say anything else, anything at all?"

The Little Brother thought hard; he knew there was something else that he was supposed to remember. He closed his eyes and recollected every moment between the time he stepped out of the palace and the time when they brought him to that room. He opened his eyes and said, "Tonight. There is something planned for tonight. That's why they brought me here instead of leaving me unconscious on the street. They wanted to be careful till tonight." He then stood up and asked the Elder Brother, "Have you captured any of them? Can we question them?"

"No, they all had those damned poison around their necks." At the Little Brother's worried face, he quickly added, "But we observed them before attacking and noticed that the villager didn't have one with him. So we tried to not hurt him much."

"He wasn't a great fighter anyway," the Third Brother said. "We held him off easily, but the men with him guessed our game, and one of them delivered a blow to his head. He is unconscious but is breathing. We locked up the bodies of the bandits in the house for proof and bound the villager to be taken to the Medica."

The Little Brother sat down again, "He might not recover fast enough for us to question him. I wonder if the Devil made any progress. What could have been planned for tonight?" he asked and looked up at the Brothers. But they were all as clueless as he was.

46. A Queen's Stage

She waited for him like always, ready and mute, sitting on their bed. He rushed into the room like always, and with a simple nod to her, picked his clothes and headed for a bath. One last time, she thought, as she curbed yet another caustic remark. That was the first lesson she had learnt from her father, even while she was forging her first piece of jewelry—keep your mouth shut and your emotion unknown, reveal only as much as needed. For a short while, when she got married, she had forgotten her lessons and it broke her heart. She had felt numb and powerless when her father died. But with her marriage, she had slowly learnt to enclose herself in her grief and emerged a stronger person. How ironic, she thought, that on her first night as the queen of Jalika, all her plans to ruin the kingdom should bear fruit.

She still remembered the day the dead king had asked her as a ransom to allow her family to flee, and her selfish brothers abandoned her to him. The bandits thought that they could entice her with the prospect of reuniting her family; what a joke. She hated her family, almost as much as she hated the unified kingdom of Jalika, whose foundations were laid on her father's grave. Her father had taught her to live strong and alone, but it was her husband who filled her blood with that truth of survival. And Veera, well, he understood that.

She saw her husband enter the room again. Before he could put on his dull grey vest, she pointed to the new green one she had put out for him on the bed. He smiled at her, in his usual condescending way like he was indulging her in a childish whim, and picked up the vest. She wanted to rage at him right then, but she held back. He would see his father's dreams crumble, just like she had, and he would go down in his royal clothes with the realization that his dear kingdom was brought down with mineral from the same mines where he loved to spend the most part of his life.

He is unusually silent today, she thought, as he motioned to her that they should leave. Was he already regretting his decision to take the throne, she wondered. Good, that would add to her pleasure. She had hatched a terrific plan to incapacitate the king so he wouldn't interfere with her plans. But those stupid bandits hadn't managed to execute her well-laid instructions, and in their ignorance, had killed the king. She had worried that the shrewd minister would take up the role, but by the end of the day, her husband had come to their room with a tired expression and told her that he was doing it. Now as she walked with him towards the well-lit and well-decorated inner gardens, she wondered whether she should have planned for the killing of his sisters. But losing the royal family may bring sympathy for Jalika rather than the wrath of the two nations for laying out the stage for a war that might as well ruin the kingdom.

The minister, the chief of guard Nayak, and a couple of other council members were already waiting for them when they arrived, and her husband immediately left her to join them. She did not mind it; let them murmur secretively. Soon the few officials from the First Nation would arrive and they would notice it with suspicion. She turned and her eyes scanned the servants setting the long dinner table. It was not necessary, she wanted to tell them. Then she looked around, ignoring them all. She had suggested a small addition to the plan, and she wanted a signal from her maid that all was ready. Nothing could go wrong, this was her final play and she had taken great pains in setting the stage.

She saw the maid on the other side and observed her as she walked toward her. That one was a snake but could be handled easily once you knew how to avoid the fangs. The maid walked toward the small chairs placed to the side where the party was to be served with refreshments before dinner. There were four round tables there, two for the hosts and two for the visitors. One of the hosts' tables was small, just for the king and the queen. Near that table, she saw the maid pause and do something. She smiled infinitesimally and turned away. If everything went according to plan, in the ensuing chaos, she would stab her husband with the engraved hunter's knife from the minister's beloved collection. The bandits had informed her to return to her chambers after that, from where they would collect her and guide her in leaving the palace. But she had her own plans; she would follow the prince to the Medica as a wife should, but there, she would abandon him just like the many times he did to her and escape with Veera.

The maid came to join her and they both gestured the king, the minister, and the council members to be seated. They all picked a glass of the drink being served and started talking when the maid left and returned saying that the visiting officials would be arriving shortly. Her heart raced with anticipation; her moment had finally come. She wished the dead king was alive just to witness her triumph over his carefully built establishment. With her right hand, she picked her glass while the left one groped for the knife underneath her chair. Then, with a knife in her hand, she too stood up along with the others.

She saw the first couple enter, along with their designated escort. It was Merin and his wife, Adola, the unintentional aides in her plan. Her eyes searched for the brooch that she had asked all women to wear on their clothing next to their hearts. When she didn't find it on Adola, her heart went wild in panic. Her eyes swung up and down the sari she had gifted to the woman, but the brooch was nowhere to be seen. Visibly angry, she looked at her maid, who was staring at the escort instead. As she turned to see what the maid was staring at, her vision followed the exact trajectory of the arrow that hit the escort in her heart, just beside the brooch, as her scream of denial pierced the silent evening air. Soon, all the escorts were hit in quick succession, and deadly silence ensued as everyone stood rooted to their spots. She was heaving for breaths now, and she looked around wildly, thinking it was a bad dream. But she had already noticed that an evident gap had been created around her, and that her husband and the minister were observing her intently. She looked at the maid and took a step in that direction, but an arrow struck the maid right in her heart, and she fell down convulsing.

It was unfair, she thought, that she was forsaken of her justice once again. She took a few steps towards the maid's body and someone on her left moved, as if to grab her. She dropped her glass and whipped the knife in her hand around. He backed off right away and she didn't linger on him to recognize the face. She reached her maid and bent down to her wound where the poison entered her heart. Her eyes finally stopped on the bloody three-knifed arrow that she had heard so much about. She pulled it out of the maid's body and looked at the knives that dripped blood.

She looked up at her husband and saw him looking at her with no expression on his face. Just like my husband, she thought, and turned to look at the minister. He was looking at her with a pitiful expression, the same one that the dead king had carried when he came to take her away from her father's mansion. Rage filled her mind, and she stood up fiercely. Everyone took a step toward her, but her husband did not move. She looked him in the eye and then punched the knives into her heart in one solid motion. The frozen face of her husband was the last thing she saw before she collapsed to her death.

47. The Devil's Tale

The Devil watched from the shadows as the queen went down. Everyone stood unmoving, some in absolute shock, some in realization of their fears. She looked at the king's face as he stared at his wife's body. When Angla had taken their findings to him, the minister had sat down the king and Nayak to explain the facts with all available proof. As they digested the news, he had moved to meet Merin and Riccham. He had told them the plan and gave them the assurance that they would not come to harm.

Her head throbbed still, but the Devil was finally able to laugh at her own stupidity for not being on alert when she was in the dark room at Veera's house. Veera had a kind of desperation about him, but he had neither the courage nor the strength to kill. At least she had waited until Veera's muscle man left the place before she went to explore the house. She might be smart and quick with her movements, but sometimes sheer force can do a lot of damage. After she had collapsed, Veera had locked the room and left. He hadn't stopped to bind her as he had already been in wait to set fire to the house, which he did minutes later. The hit to her head had been soft as both his hands and the log were slippery with oil. If she hadn't gone down like she did, there was no telling what he might've done. She had wanted him to escape so that she could find out his next move. But what she hadn't expected was getting locked in a room with smoke and fire about.

As the smoke hit her, she had wrapped herself in a thick blanket that she found on the small bed in the room and picked up the log that Veera had used to hit her. She had used the same log to break open the door and ran out blindly towards the open air. The hall had been covered in flames by then and the smoke and the heat had nearly choked her to death. She had barely managed to break open the other two doors to get to the stairs and rush down. After she had taken a few deep breaths, she had gone around the house to the front. The horse carriage had still been there but its carriage was locked. From there, she had seen the distant image of Veera walking down the trail. She had wondered why he did not take the carriage. He was on his way to do something where he did not need the added baggage, she had guessed. Perhaps the muscle man was ordered to return and take the carriage to wherever he took the bullock cart, she had concluded. Then as quickly as her legs could carry, she had gone after Veera.

After almost an hour, he had slowed down near the village, just beyond the plantations after the palace gardens. He had seemed a little unsure at first, but after a few turns he stopped at a spot on the edge of a street and stared at one of the five huts that stood there. She too had stopped and observed him from a distance. He had walked close to the hut on the extreme right and stood listening to the voices inside. Then he had gone around it from the back and reached the hut next to it on the right that was partially covered to the Devil by the earlier one. She had shifted her position as well to get a view of him again. He had peeked into the second hut intently, his eyes darting from left to right slowly. He had then come back his way, entered the main road, and walked towards the muddy, stony path between the plantations. Deciding to check the huts again later, she had followed him once again.

He had reached the small fish market near the port and walked alongside it to reach a lodge. It was a shabby two-storey building, and he had spoken to someone outside the main door on the road. Had the Devil not been already familiar with the place, she wouldn't have realized the nature of the building. After a while, both the men had gone inside, shutting the door behind them. It would have been too risky to do anything there and she would be wasting valuable time by simply waiting for him to come out. So, she had picked out a small note, wrote a message on it for the Brothers to come and keep an eye on Veera, gave one last look at the building, and left. She had gone back to the fish market, hired a young girl to send out her message, and picked her trail back to the huts.

When she had reached there, she saw a young boy, who she later found out to be the helper of the queen's maid, leave the first hut and approach the second one. A few minutes later, he had come out and entered the first hut only to emerge again with bundles of what she had guessed to be food wrapped in leaves. She had moved closer to the second hut, but not too close. Instead, she had taken out her spyglass and peeked in. Other than the boy, there had been five other men in the room. She had braved a few inches closer and stopped when she could hear the conversation faintly. The boy had been talking to the men as he served their food.

"... won't get another meal till the job is done and you are out, without falling under anyone's eyes. So, eat well. Have you memorized the drawing on the wall? We can't be carrying any parchment with us; there won't be any use for it in the dark."

At those words, the Devil had focused her glass on the walls of the room and found the same drawing on three of the walls, a white round circle with an emblem from the First Nation. It was made by the First Nation's officials to celebrate a small victory over the Second Nation at the borders near the Stana River up in the north. And the Second Nation had vowed to kill anyone wearing that symbol. The Devil had given out a small laugh at the simple risk of misusing the symbol and then had searched the room for what she was looking. And sure enough, there she had found the arrows that were stolen from the visitor's trunk.

The five men had moved and behaved like tribesmen, though they had been wearing black garments. They must be huntsmen from the tribes, she had decided, the kind that hunted since childhood and could hit any animal in the eye from a long distance. She had left her spot then and reached the village. She had found a young boy this time to carry her message to the Brothers to find out about five missing huntsmen from the Koli tribe on the deep end of the Chama forest. Then she had gone back to the huts and waited. As the sun began to go down and the air became chilly, the men had finally stepped out of their hut. The boy had been carrying a lantern held high, and the rest of them had been carrying their wooden bows and a wrapped cloth that showed the ends of the arrows, two on each man.

Like Veera, they too had turned towards the plantations but used the small uneven trails right in the middle of the plantations instead. They had made their way toward the palace wall at the edge of the gardens, where a few tools and store rooms in the end merged into cleaning rooms and quarters for the servants in the palace. There, they had waited, with the boy craning his neck to look for something inside the wall. Following them closely and keeping them in her line of sight, the Devil too had waited.

48. False Promises

Angla instructed a female member from his young squad to wrap the queen's body and move it to her quarters. He then turned to the other female members who arrived then and told them to clear out the other bodies. As the minister and the king left the place, Nayak stepped in to request the visiting couples from the First Nation to move to the hall. No one expected the queen to go down like she did, and those present were still reeling from the shock of her death.

Angla looked at the queen's body as it was moved and wondered if she deserved to die like that. Maybe she is peaceful now, he thought, considering how she led a disruptive life. He turned to the maid's body lying beside the queen's and then to the dead bodies of the escorts that were being cleared out. Those women were a terrible surprise. When Angla found out that the maid had picked five of her personal cronies to escort the officials to dinner, the Elder Brother immediately recognized them. They were the same women who posed as midwives and were responsible for the death of several babies in the smaller islands. Though they hadn't come under the notice of the palace yet, word about their atrocities spread among villagers in the islands. Drawings of the women circled about in the villages and that was how the Elder Brother had known of them. Angla could only imagine and shudder at the havoc they would've wreaked in the chaos had the queen's plan gone through.

Angla noticed the brooches on the bodies of the escorts and smiled at the simple idea that the Devil had suggested. It had been easy to convince the hunters to fall in with their plan; all he had to do was inform them the truth that their families were being held captured by the bandits. After they had received the Devil's message, the Second Brother and the Third Brother had left for the hunters' tribe and found out the situation.

They had immediately sent a note to Angla informing him of the same and asked him to send reinforcements. The information had angered the hunters who had already started to doubt the promise of the bandits because of the maid's behavior. They agreed to do the dirty deed only because the bandits had promised to protect their tribe from a terrible epidemic that affected many people there. Angla easily guessed that the epidemic could very well have been spread by the bandits themselves and that there was no cure. The bandits might've captured the families so that when the truth came out, the hunters would not strike against them or reveal their involvement. Angla had convinced the hunters about the true nature of the bandits and assuaged their fears by sending his people to the Brothers to handle the situation for them back home.

Angla sighed and looked up. Merin and his wife Adola, who were following Nayak out, nodded to him, and he gave them a salute. Their trust and help had made the countermeasures for the night successful.

He had been crawling on the roofs of the unused servant quarters trying to locate the maid who had disappeared there when he saw a twinkle outside the palace wall, just behind the cleaning rooms. He had spotted the hunters then, standing behind a young man with a lantern. As he crawled a bit further up, he had noticed the Devil wave at him from a short distance behind them. After nodding at her, he had watched as the young man made a pattern of noises. A moment later, he had heard an answering pattern from the inside the wall and suddenly noticed a shadow moving there. At one spot, the shadow had stopped and groped for something on the wall. He had realized that it was the maid and watched keenly as she pulled out a circular portion of the wall using a tiny handle. A gaping hole appeared there and the young man had herded the hunters inside before following suit. Then the maid had closed the hole and led the men inside. Angla had kept an eye on the maid as the Devil disappeared to enter the palace near the gardens.

Angla had waited till the Devil approached the quarters, and then he directed her towards the standalone cleaning rooms that were built for the use of the elderly, where the maid had taken the hunters and her little errand boy. There was only one way from there toward the edge of the quarters, and once the Devil had made for it, he had climbed down from the roof and followed her. By the time he had reached the quarters, the Devil had already found the room the maid was in. There, while waiting for the maid to leave, they had informed each other of their findings. He had told her about the dinner and she had told him about how she came to follow the hunters. Then they had decided that the Devil should go speak to Merin's wife, Adola, as she was the only one the queen had spoken to about the dinner, and Angla would keep an eye on the room.

Angla had watched as the maid left with her errand boy in tow and knew that the young man he had posted nearby would follow her. Then he had waited a bit longer before entering the room to speak to the hunters. There had been confusion at first and then fright, but he had immediately launched into a monologue on how they could get free from the clutches of the bandits. He had then explained to them about the real nature of the bandits and then assured them that they would come up with a plan. After they had agreed, Angla too went to Merin's house and met the Devil there. The Devil had found out that the queen had given Adola a brooch, which bore the same pattern that she had seen on the walls of the hut. The hunters had already told Angla that they were supposed to hit those with the mark using the arrows from the Second Nation that were coated with the poison stolen from the palace. So, after conferring with the Devil once, Angla had gone straight to the minister.

Merin had wanted the evidence to come out in the open on its own in front of the other officials from the First Nation so that there would be no doubt about their claims. Except for a small look of surprise when Angla mentioned the Devil, the king had remained silent. But Nayak had suggested that the king would want more proof to believe that his wife was the evil mastermind. The Elder Brother had come in to meet Angla just then and had informed him that he had followed Veera from the port to the Medica and had captured him when he was lurking there secretly. When Angla had gone to question him, Veera fought wildly to escape and absolutely refused to say a word after they subjugated him. As there was not much time left, Angla had set the Little Brother on guard to watch over him and left the place. He had then called over the Elder Brother and the Devil to meet with the king, the minister, and Nayak so they could come up with a plan to handle the situation.

The hunters had told him that the brooches were a last minute idea and when the Elder Brother had informed about them the escorts, they had decided that they should let the escorts wear the brooches instead, so that the hunters could carry out their instructions without alarming anyone. After the escorts go down, they had planned to capture the maid and her helper and interrogate them along with the hunters for the truth. They had also ordered the hunters to shoot if anyone at the dinner looked to cause any harm. One of the hunters, in his anger towards the maid who had threatened him with his family's death, had fired the arrow when the queen had moved towards her. They had expected the queen to cover up her involvement in the plan, but in a moment of heartbreak she had killed herself, thus proving without a doubt all their suspicions to be true.

49. Towards Tomorrow

The maid's helper, who had been waiting to take the hunters back the same way they had come in, was captured by Angla's man who was following the maid. A few minutes later, the boy was confessing to everything in front of the king, the minister, Nayak, Merin, other officials from the First Nation, Riccham, and a few officials from the Second Nation who rode out early from the Second Palace on the Second Brother's request. Angla spoke to the group after that, so did Merin and his wife, and then Riccham, the Elder Brother, and finally the hunters too came forward once Angla assured them that their families were safe.

After that, Angla went to see Veera, the queen's main accomplice apart from the maid. As Angla and the Elder Brother approached the room where he was held, they found the Little Brother sitting on a chair outside the room with the door open. He looked at them questioningly, and Angla immediately gave him the news that their plan had gone well. Angla explained to them what had happened at dinner, and as he mentioned the queen's death, they heard a small scream from inside the room. They went in to see the captive wailing as if he was in terrible pain. They knew a part of Veera's story from the Devil, who had seen the portraits in his room.

The despaired man in front of him looked much different to Angla than the one he had seen a while ago, before the dinner. But then, the man had just learnt about the queen's death and had lost all hope of ever escaping the place with her. He first shouted at them that they were lying to him, but when Angla told him that he could see her body for himself and explained to him the manner in which she killed herself, he fell back into his chair staring at Angla. He remained silent after that, and when Angla slowly asked him about the queen, he told them the whole story without much provocation.

The most shocking thing that Veera told them was that the queen had once planned her husband's murder at the mines. Even though it failed, she didn't despair because no one at the palace seemed to connect it back to her. Somehow, the bandits had learnt about it and had approached her through her maid. By then, the maid had already been working for her for some time and had been sparking hatred for her husband and his family in her mind. Though it made it easy for the queen to agree to escape with him, Veera had not been happy with her alliance with the bandits. After the old king's death, he had begged her to leave with him, but she wasn't ready to let her husband and his sisters live like royals while she would escape like a prisoner and seek refuge elsewhere.

Angla recollected the accident in the mines. The prince had come home then, with minor injuries, and stayed back until he recovered. It was possible that he had a nagging suspicion about his wife, Angla thought. After that, the frequency of his visits to the palace had increased, though Angla had dismissed it at the time thinking that it was due the ongoing negotiations on the peace treaty. But now he realized that the prince had not attended any council meetings, only discussed terms once in a while with the king and the minister. Angla gave a look to the Brothers and then turned to Veera. He asked Veera about his relationship with the queen and it made him launch into another fit of weary talking fractured with gulping breaths.

"I was a student of the queen's father," Veera told them, "when my parents worked for that family. My father was injured in the war and our family had to escape from Bora in order to survive. Soon after that, my father passed away, and my mother and I, knowing only to work in a smithy, went to work for a jeweler. After working there for several years, I inherited that place from the jeweler as he was widowed and did not have any children. However, he had a young niece who came to live with him in his last years, and on my dying mother's insistence, I married her. I lived as a jeweler in the same village with my wife for three years before she and our newborn child passed away due to bad health, within a span of few weeks from each other. To escape from my grief, I sold everything there and returned to Bora two years ago, the only other familiar place to me. It was then that I found out what had happened to the queen since her father died. I searched for this old friend of their family and got the details from her. She told me that she had tried to keep in touch with the merchant's daughter after she was moved to the palace but the girl refused to talk to her. Hoping to find out more, I found a house near the palace with an unused smithy ready for me to work. When I heard that the prince's wife was looking for smiths for her own workshop inside the palace, I went to meet her.

"She instantly recognized the symbol I used in a sample piece of jewelry and sought me out to speak of old times. We recollected our childhood spent in her father's workshop learning jewelry making and refreshed our memories of our language of secret shapes of metal. After realizing that I too had lost all my family, she talked to me more freely and told me about her mercenary life in the palace. It was from me that she learnt that only one of her brothers was alive and that he wouldn't be interested in her at all. She had already guessed at the double edge sword that dealing with the bandits was, and I gave her the much needed confirmation. We made her escape plan then, and after that she insisted that we shouldn't be seen together, considering the risks. So she hired me as one of the smiths who would provide her designs from the outside and we decided only to communicate using symbols in jewelry."

Once Veera concluded his story, the Elder Brother gave him a glass of water to drink. After he agreed to confess everything he knew in front of the council and the visiting officials, they left him there and stepped out. Angla thanked the Brothers for their work, not just in capturing and securing Veera but also with everything else for the past seven days. Then he mentioned to the Elder Brother an idea that had been forming in his head. He knew that once the peace treaty was signed and the palace achieved stability, the minister would want to retire from his position, and Nayak would be asked to fulfill his role. Then he, Angla, might be asked to take up the role of his chief. He was not sure about the responsibilities of the council, but with the help of the Brotherhood, if they accept to be his aides, he could leave some ground work to them and deal with the politics himself.

The Elder Brother thanked him for the offer and said that he would discuss it with the other Brothers and let him know their decision. Since their identity was already revealed in the palace, he considered that it wouldn't be a big burden for them to accept the role offered by Angla. Angla nodded at that, bid them farewell, and went to see if he could finally talk to the minister or Nayak about the next day.

50. The Deadly Peace

As the Little Brother waited in the audience, he thought about the Devil and smiled. What a force to be reckoned with, that woman. He knew that if it wasn't for her, they wouldn't have been able to avert the disaster that would've crumbled Jalika. Even with all he knew of her, he didn't expect her to pull the disappearance act so soon. He had believed that his time with her warranted at least a farewell message, but when he returned to his Medica room for one last time late in the night, he knew in his heart that it would never come.

It was a bright morning and he was glad that he decided to sit deep inside the tent, which shielded him both from the sun and from questioning eyes. The knowledge that something odd had happened at the queen's dinner and that she had died had spread quickly and people were eager for more news. His swollen cheek had drawn many eyes already and he had chosen to lie low till it was healed.

People had started arriving early in the morning to secure a place as close to the stage as possible to witness the signing of the treaty. Even with moments for the officials to arrive, many people were still coming in. The dais was still unoccupied and the Little Brother saw Angla on the ground beside it. He was talking to different people, passing orders to some standing far from the stage, and his alert eyes scanned the grounds even as his face looked bruised from lack of sleep.

If the Devil had a tinge of indifference when it came to matters that didn't concern her, Angla had a sense of calmness about him; nothing could break his composure and he rolled along with things as they came. Still, he was a good, duty-bound man who learnt and adapted well and would make a good chief, the Little Brother concluded. As he observed the man carrying out his duty, the Little Brother recollected the conversation with him the night before when Angla had come to visit him in his room.

He hadn't been able to sleep and had been staring at the palace when Angla came in and sat by his side.

"Unable to sleep?" Angla had asked him then, "What are you frowning about?"

"I keep thinking about the Devil. She has already left, hasn't she?"

"It takes a few times to be neither happy nor disappointed with her. Don't worry, she'll return enough times for you to get used to it."

"So you know her well then?"

"Knew her well, I don't anymore. She has changed much over the years and we grew apart. But it has all been for the good, I've never respected her more."

There had been a calm silence after that as they both stared out the window and then the Little Brother had asked him softly, "Tell me about her."

Angla had taken out his pipe, waited for the Little Brother to do the same, and lit them both. Then he had asked the Little Brother, "What do you want to know?"

"What's her name?"

Angla had thrown back his head in laughter and patted the Little Brother's shoulder. Then he had coughed to stop choking on his own smoke and answered him.

"I don't know her name. I doubt anyone here in the palace knows either." Angla's voice had dropped low then, but looking at his calm and tired face, somehow the Little Brother knew that he was not telling him the truth. Before he could ask any questions, Angla had continued quickly, "The little devil, the king had called her when he met her the first time, and that was how everyone referred to her afterwards."

"So, she never told anyone her name? How did she come here in the first place?"

"She was here only for a few years. Our king, the then prince, found her. He used to accompany his father on his sailing expeditions to discover new islands and meet new tribes deep in the forests. After a while, he started sailing on his own. On one such day, he found her on a shore.

"She was alone and was frantically trying to get his attention. She had been on that shore for about two days before he found her. She was from a tribe on the other side of the hill, deep into the island, and she had climbed out alone. She wasn't speaking the common language and it took him a while to understand her. Her tribe never left the small forest on the other side of the hill. When a demonic disease was killing everyone in their tribe, she had begged the people to cross the hill and leave the place. But she was only six, too young to convince them, and the tribe was too scared to cross the hill. So, she crossed it alone to save her own self and to prove that it was safe, but she lost her way and found herself out of the forest, on a shore, with no idea where to go next or how to go back.

"When the prince had found her, she had asked him to come with her to the other side of the hill to rescue her tribe members. But on hearing about the epidemic, he asked her then to go with him to his father first and then he would send in someone to rescue her tribe. But by the time the king and his men found their tribe, everyone was dead. She, who had pestered the king till he left for her tribe, took one look at his face when he came back and did not ask him a single question about what he found there. He brought her to the school that had just been started by the palace and she lived there after that."

"She loved the prince then, the man who rescued her. That's why you wouldn't believe her when she suspected his wife?"

"She had attached herself too strongly to him and that obsession was her only curse for as long as I knew her. The dead king realized it even if his son never did. The last time I remember seeing her in the palace was the night she went away for long. She might have, in her naïve understanding of her feelings for him, decided to marry him and had approached his father, who over the years had come to be her friend and mentor. But he understood her too well and knew that life in palace would stifle her. They had words and he eventually made her see. She went away then, for the first time. When I didn't hear from her for a long time, I thought her to be dead, because why wouldn't she contact me? But, I later found her out and even met her a few times briefly. She was changed. Oh, she was still the same girl that I remembered her to be, focused, determined, and wild. But there was a cloak of indifference around her that I couldn't penetrate. I do not know if her love for the prince ever died, all I know is that after she was brought to the school, she never grieved for her lost home, her lost tribe, or her lost family, but she always remembered. And wherever she went when she left here, and whatever she did there, changed her, changed her so much that the dead king who used to consider her his beloved student, transformed her into his secret weapon."

People all around the Little Brother started to murmur excitedly and he looked towards the stage. He could see that the officials had arrived and had taken seat on the chairs laid out for them. The minister stood up and started speaking. The spokespersons placed at each tent across the grounds read out the same words from a parchment.

"It is with great sorrow we inform you that the queen has passed away last night with a sudden heart ailment. It is a blow to our palace, too soon after the king's death. It is only to keep their dream for peace in Jalika alive that we continue to move forward with the Peace Events as we had originally planned. In honor of their memory and in the surety of a great bond between Jalika and the two great nations of Khaga, I request the peace treaty be signed."

At this, the king of Jalika, and the two officials on either side of him stood up. The minister picked another parchment to read out from, and then as the people of Jalika waited with bated breath, the two officials nodded at the king and punched their seals onto the parchment that the minister was holding. The minister handed the parchment over to the king, who looked at it carefully and punched his seal.

CPSIA information can be obtained
at www.ICGtesting.com
Printed in the USA
LVOW12s1139190416
484302LV00001B/101/P